SPANISH EYES

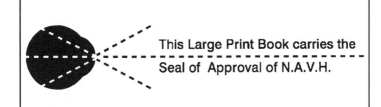

This Large Print Book carries the
Seal of Approval of N.A.V.H.

SPANISH EYES

JACKIE GRIFFEY

THORNDIKE PRESS
A part of Gale, Cengage Learning

GALE
CENGAGE Learning·

Detroit • New York • San Francisco • New Haven, Conn • Waterville, Maine • London

GALE
CENGAGE Learning

ALL RIGHTS RESERVED
This novel is a work of fiction. Names, characters, places and incidents are either the product of the author's imagination, or, if real, used fictitiously.
Thorndike Press® Large Print Clean Reads.
The text of this Large Print edition is unabridged.
Other aspects of the book may vary from the original edition.
Set in 16 pt. Plantin.
Printed on permanent paper.

LIBRARY OF CONGRESS CATALOGING-IN-PUBLICATION DATA

Griffey, Jackie.
    Spanish eyes / by Jackie Griffey.
        p. cm. — (Thorndike Press large print clean reads)
    ISBN-13: 978-1-4104-0886-0 (hardcover : alk. paper)
    ISBN-10: 1-4104-0886-8 (hardcover : alk. paper)
    1. Mexicans—Texas—Fiction. 2. Missing persons—Fiction. 3. Large type books. I. Title.
    PS3607.R544S63 2008
    813'.6—dc22   2008031011

Published in 2008 by arrangement with Tekno Books.

Printed in the United States of America
1 2 3 4 5 6 7 12 11 10 09 08

Dedicated to my husband and family, who ate all those Crock-Pot dinners and pizzas so I could work, and to friends and fellow writers who critique and encourage and point me in the right direction when my research hits a snag. You're essential and appreciated as well as loved. Thank you.

CHAPTER ONE

Eleana's big brown eyes gleamed with happiness as she carefully dialed the number she had copied from the phone book. She tucked it neatly back into her purse with one hand as she listened to the phone ring.

"*Por favor,* please." She breathlessly switched to English when she heard the woman answer. "I need to contact my brother who is working for you. To tell him I am here in Las Flores now. I was to contact him through you as soon as I got here."

"What is his name?"

"Carlos Castillo. He has worked for you before." Eleana smiled into the phone and waited.

She didn't have long to wait. As she listened to the efficient female voice, which had answered so promptly, Eleana's face lost its happiness and worry lines appeared. Her stomach contracted as if from a hard blow as she realized what the woman was saying.

Too surprised and disappointed to speak, Eleana simply mumbled, "*Gracias.* Thank you." She hung up, feeling lost.

Carlos was not there, the woman had said. Not there? How could he not be there? Happiness was replaced with a desperate resolve. She must find Carlos. Eleana prayed he was all right. But where could he be? All kinds of dangerous things that could have happened to her older brother went through her mind like a horror movie.

With a cold feeling in the pit of her stomach, Eleana felt frightened, lost and alone in a strange place. She had just arrived to work; no wonder she felt lost. But even though he had come here before, Carlos too was a stranger here. He had encouraged her while she was waiting for her papers, told her he would be waiting for her. She was to contact him where he would be working. It was all arranged. She shook her head. This did not make sense.

Thinking back over the letters Carlos had written and the times he had talked to her about coming to Las Flores to work, Eleana tried to think of where she might look for him, places he might go.

She turned away from the unhelpful

phone with an urgency only fear for a loved one can generate. She must find him!

Oliver Avery entered the shopping mall and stopped abruptly, his artist's eyes caught and held by the woman on the mezzanine above him.

There's a work of art, a live one!

Oliver Avery was arrested midstep. Caught in a spell, he stood as if his sneakers were nailed to the floor of the mall. He stood gazing up in awe at the lovely woman on the mezzanine. Beautiful as a perfect statue come to life, in soft, olive skin. He gazed at her just right figure, her dark hair, her beautiful face, and her dark eyes. It was her eyes that held his attention. She stood very still, looking intently down on the crowd below her.

To Oliver, she looked like all the descriptions of Latin beauties and Madonnas rolled into one.

Spanish eyes! Oliver breathed to himself, remembering the song.

The object of his wondering gaze stood on the mezzanine in front and almost directly above him. She seemed completely unaware of him or the throng of people around her. Those dark eyes were drawn only to the faces below. They were intent on

9

the people entering the wide double doors. The main entrance into the mall was directly behind him.

As Oliver watched, she concentrated on each face as if committing it to memory. Then, laying her small hand on the rail in front of her, she leaned forward a little. Those dark eyes were still questing, questing, questing, looking for someone.

Suddenly a dry feeling made Oliver aware that his mouth was hanging open in an unbecoming gape. He shut it quickly with an inaudible sigh.

She doesn't see me, or anyone else for that matter. I wonder what all that concentration is about. Who it is she's looking for?

A wave of jealousy washed over his heart. He only knew that sought-for one was lucky. That man, that woman or child. He had to know more. He had to know her. To touch her, to hold her and comfort her, to take away that desperate look. He had to meet her.

He had been standing like an extra column in the middle of the foot traffic as he looked up, spellbound and motionless. He looked around him, aware again of people flowing around him. One or two who passed gave him an annoyed glance as they looked back.

Then, apparently giving up her search, the

10

dark vision above him straightened. If she saw him staring, she gave no indication she'd seen him as she scanned once more the entering crowds. She turned and went down the shop-lined floor above him, disappearing as if by magic in the crowd of people. The fleeting vision of her had etched itself in his memory.

Oliver, with his artist's appreciation, lost a few seconds noting she looked as pretty going as she did coming. Then his feet obeyed the order to follow. To find her. He had no idea how he would introduce himself when he did catch up with her, or anything else constructive. He only knew he had to find her.

The escalator was too slow. Oliver hurried as fast as he could to the stairs. He took the steps two or three at a time with his long legs. He was panting a little when he got to the top and looked around for his dark-eyed dream girl.

In panic and disappointment he swiveled his neck, his eyes searching the throng of people as hers had. But she had disappeared like a dream that couldn't be held. Or a wave that rushed back to the sea before you could catch it. The dark beauty was nowhere in sight.

Oliver looked in all the shop windows and

doors. He tried going into the shops or boutiques where he thought she might have gone. There was no sign of her in the shops he peered into or the long, wide hall outside the shops.

Hope leaped again when he sighted a lingerie shop farther down. He took a quick, furtively embarrassed look around before going to peer intently through its windows. This shop rivaled Victoria's Secret, or maybe Frederick's of Hollywood. He felt the flush of embarrassment on his face as he turned away.

She was not there. She must have gone back down while he searched. His shoulders drooped with disappointment. He consoled himself with the thought he had no idea what to say to her even if he had caught up with her. He went back to where he had seen her standing. It was the best place to look, to find someone. He stood a few seconds looking down from the mezzanine. He wondered briefly if she might have gone down on the escalator as he had taken the stairs. But there was no head in the throng below him that looked like his dark Madonna.

Going back down, he used the escalator this time. He could see the shop where he got most of his art supplies. He was teaching an "Intro" course in oil painting this summer. His job teaching at the Las Flores College paid well enough, but the money from the summer course would enable him to put something in his investment fund with enough left over for a trip or whatever he wanted to do with it, before the fall term began.

The craft shop was not very far from the stairway and Oliver was soon concentrating on the list of things he wanted to get. Then, glancing up, he saw the back of a dark head that looked like the beautiful stranger. He dropped the things he'd picked up on the shelf and hurried out just in time to see the lady turn her head to greet someone.

She was not his dark beauty with the Spanish eyes.

Oliver's beautiful Madonna had noticed him, but her head was too full of questions and growing concern to spare him more than the briefest notice.

Her Spanish eyes had reason to be troubled. None of the faces Eleana peered down on looked even a little like Carlos. She pictured her brother's handsome face, excited and smiling at her as they'd talked of both of them working in Las Flores. Her heart ached for her big brother, sure now there must be something wrong.

She thought of calling the hospital, but discarded the idea. If he had been hurt, he had identification. The hospital would have notified the family. She was at a loss where to begin.

Eleana's troubled mind tried to find an explanation but there was none. She knew her brother well. Carlos would not have just gone away without a word. He would have let his family know where he was — if he could! She must find him.

After that first call, Eleana had called back the place he was supposed to be. There must be some mistake. She had been too shocked to say anything at such unacceptable news. The second time Eleana had tried to explain to the feminine voice.

"But I was told he would be there. The name, his name is Castillo, Carlos Castillo." Eleana said it slowly and carefully, spelled the name.

"I'll look again," the pleasant voice told her. Eleana held the phone and heard the rustle of paper as she waited.

"No," the note of finality was audible. Still very nice, but it sounded very certain now. "There is no Carlos Castillo on my list of workers here."

Eleana's brows drew together. She didn't

say anything, picturing a long list of names in the woman's hand.

"You might check again and see if you got the name of the place right." The voice was sympathetic.

At a loss how to answer, Eleana had at least managed to say, "Thank you. I will check and see that I have the name right."

Eleana was troubled as she replaced the receiver the second time. *Carlos, my brother, where are you? I know this place is the one you worked for before. I know this is the right name.*

She resolved to call and talk to Raquel, her cousin at home. Raquel could go to Carlos's wife, Carlotta, and ask the name of the place Carlos was working, just to be sure. But she was sure. Where could he be? What could have happened? And why had he not told them? Her only comfort was the family she knew she could reach.

Carlotta will know the name. Perhaps I did have it wrong. Her heart warmed, picturing her sister-in-law, Carlotta. And Juan. Juan was her and Carlos's young brother. Carlotta was with child. Juan was nearly grown now, and was staying with Carlotta while Carlos went away to work. He was feeling quite a man who took his responsibility seriously. He was already calling himself Tío Juan.

I should call and ask how Carlotta is doing anyway. This little one is the first one for her and Carlos. I am glad Juan is staying with her while Carlos is away. She will know where he is. Eleana's dark eyes lost their worried look. Thinking of Carlotta and Juan, she smiled, feeling better.

But Carlotta and Juan were not safely at home the way Eleana pictured them. At that very moment they were running as if their lives depended on it, fear lending wings to their feet.

"Dogs! Carlotta, I hear dogs!"

Fear gripped Juan's heart but he kept running as fast as he could.

Carlotta did not even glance over her shoulder as she ran faster.

Her arms cradled her abdomen as she ran. Her bag was slung over her shoulder so it would hang behind her.

"It is not much farther now, Juan," Carlotta managed to gasp. Her breath was getting short. She had to encourage Juan, to keep him running as fast as he could.

"The barking, the patrol and their dogs are back below the sand hills," Carlotta assured him. "They cannot see us. It is not much farther now, only a little way —"

On they went. Juan was fourteen years old and trying so hard to be a man. Carlos was depending on him to take care of Carlotta. His heart swelled with pride at his brother's confidence and pride in him. He frowned, worried and scared. Carlotta was so determined about this trip, and she was in the sixth month of her pregnancy. Both of them prayed silently as they ran, their sandals slapping the ground in a desperate rhythm.

"*There!* There, Juan. That next rise. It is not much the other side of that. We are going to make it, Juan!"

Juan's face split in a wide white grin and he ran even faster, though he hadn't thought he could.

Carlotta was running faster too. Hope lent her strength and speed as Juan prayed again for her and the *niño* she was carrying. There was no doubt in his young heart the baby would be a boy. A fine, healthy, handsome boy. He would look like his little cousin. Only more handsome, more brave . . . Juan's thoughts ran faster than his toughened, brown feet.

My nephew, pride swelled his chest. *Or my niece? No matter, I will be an uncle.* He grinned to himself, *Tío Juan!*

He glanced fearfully at Carlotta as they

topped the slight rise and started down. She was breathing heavily but she kept up the swift pace.

"Juan!" She stopped and grabbed his arm, heaving, trying to catch her breath as he stood silent and frightened beside her.

"There," she pointed toward the water. "We will go into the water there. Quickly!"

She started toward the water and Juan followed obediently. He looked cautiously around as he waded, the water up to his knees.

"We must be quick; we have to make it while the two rises protect us from the patrol."

The water wasn't cold and felt comfortingly good. The night was hot. The water was up to Juan's chest now and he couldn't move as quickly.

Carlotta was using her arms as well as her feet and was going faster than he thought she would be able to move. Neither spoke, but concentrated on moving through the shallow river water as fast as possible.

Carlotta saw Juan glance over his shoulder. They could hear the dogs but they didn't sound any closer than when Juan had first heard them.

They hurried on, moving awkwardly through the water. It comforted Juan to know the water would leave no tracks and no scent. He let Carlotta stay a little ahead of him for fear she might slip and need his support. He was wondering, as he waded and paddled with his hands, if his fingers were wrinkling like last time they came down to swim in the river, when Carlotta spoke again.

"We're nearly there. It is just around that big rock there." Carlotta pointed. "Are you all right? Is everything still there or did we lose anything? No matter. We will have plenty of time to see about that when we get there. I can see it, Juan!"

Carlotta stopped suddenly and squeezed his arm, as much for support as to stop him. "We are here, Juan," she said haltingly. She tried to get her breath and he saw how tired she was.

"But," Juan looked around them. "Where?" The river looked the same here as it did farther down, across from their house. Worried even more now, he raised his eyes to Carlotta.

"It is hidden, you can't see it," Carlotta explained. "Nobody else will be able to see it either. I found it by accident when I came here a few weeks ago. We are going to hold our breath now and go under the water and come up under that bank where those stones are."

"Carlotta?" Juan was not convinced.

"What you must do is hold your breath and go under the water. Move forward about three long steps then come back up."

Juan stood still, unmoving.

"Here." Carlotta straightened the burden on her shoulder and reached out to him. "I will hold your hand and we will go together."

She kept one hand on the strap of her shoulder bag and took his hand with the other.

Juan briefly checked the plastic bags he carried with his other hand, then announced bravely, "I am ready!"

He held his nose with the hand he had free, since all the bags were still fastened. He closed his eyes as the water closed over them.

Down they went and took the three long steps as Carlotta said. In a matter of seconds they came up and were facing each other in the dark of an underground hollow.

"I can't see, Carlotta!" Juan tried to keep the fear out of his voice.

"It's all right. I can't either right now. I'm going to move away a little. You stand very still, right here. Mind me now," Carlotta insisted. "Just as you mind Carlos."

"I will. I will stand right here. How would I know where else to go?" He fought the hysteria that edged into his words.

He heard the water splash as Carlotta moved and he tried to guess where she was. Then suddenly, there was light!

He squinted in the sudden glare. He saw Carlotta sitting on a narrow ledge with her legs dangling in the water, her bag beside her.

"Come up here quickly and sit beside me. Put the bags beside you and get as well set as you can. We must turn off the light."

He hastily joined Carlotta and put the bags beside him. He still held tightly to the straps.

Carlotta turned off the light and the dark closed in on them.

"All right?"

"Yes. The bags, too. And you are right." Juan shook his head though she couldn't see him. "No one will find us here."

Carlotta was breathing easier now. "I found this place when I was visiting nearby. I didn't tell anyone about it, not even Carlos. So it is a good hiding place."

The name of Carlos brought the memory of his big brother's face and a pang of conscience distracted him until Juan heard the dogs again.

"Listen! The dogs are coming closer!" Juan spoke softly, frightened again.

"Yes, I hear them. We had better not talk anymore until they are gone. I will feel in my bag and get us some bread to eat while we wait." He heard the plastic rattle as she searched.

They were silent, listening anxiously to the dogs coming closer.

Juan felt Carlotta's hand on his arm. It followed his arm and sleeve to his hand and put a big piece of bread in it. Neither spoke. The lap of water and their shallow breathing were the only sounds besides the excited yelps and barks of the dogs in the distance.

Fear was almost a tangible thing, but the river patrol never came very close to their hiding place. They sat in the dark, ate their bread, and listened.

Once they heard a dog splashing in the water but it sounded like it went on across the river. The Rio Grande was narrow along there.

Finally, the voices that occasionally called to each other and the barking seemed to be fading, and Carlotta said softly, "I knew there was no way to keep them from following our trail with the dogs. But by now they think we must have crossed and gone on. They are leaving."

Juan listened. He could still hear the dogs, but they were steadily growing fainter.

As they sat in the dark, their eyes grew accustomed to it and they could see a little by the refracted moonlight on the water.

"Feels good to rest a while, doesn't it?" Carlotta smiled at the dark shape of brave Tío Juan. "You are brave, like Carlos. Some day we will tell him of our journey."

"Yes, we will tell him." Juan's eyes were worried, peering into the dark around them. He pictured Carlos. Strong, handsome, good Carlos. His big brother who did everything right. His imagination showed him clearly the anger on that face. The anger that would be there if he knew where Juan and his Carlotta and his unborn child were right now. Juan's eyes tried to pierce the darkness and he shivered. His big brother's anger at him when he found out about the terrible chances he and Carlotta were taking was a fearful thing to think about. He was glad it was dark and Carlotta could not see his face.

"The water feels good. Is it safe to go on now?" he asked softly. He had a fleeting wish he could wake up in his own bed, this journey only a dangerous dream.

"First, check both the bags and I will check the one around my shoulder too."

He checked them by feeling with his hands. "All is well. There are not any leaks and the straps you put around them are holding."

"*Bueno.* Mine too. May the good Lord bless the makers of plastic bags, eh, Juan?" Carlotta laughed.

Juan nodded, forgetting she might not be able to see him. "How long do you think it will take us to get there, Carlotta?"

"Probably about three days. We will have to stop to rest and to sleep and to eat along the way. I am hoping to make it in two days, but it may be three. I have the map Carlos made when they came this way. But I don't know how fast we can go." The fear in her mind added, *Or what to expect when we get there.*

Carlotta lowered herself carefully into the water. "All right, Juan, let us go before another patrol comes along."

The thought of another patrol was enough to stir Juan to action. He jumped down from the ledge to join her.

"All right. We go!" Carlotta took his hand and they went under the water and out of the safe little grotto into the river again.

Cautiously, both of them looked in all directions. They stood very still, their heads just out of the water.

"I don't hear anything," Juan ventured hopefully.

"No, they are gone now." She rose and so did Juan, the water again striking him in his chest. He followed her across the narrow river. He held tightly to the two plastic bags, trying not to think of the anger on his big brother's face or that he would surely face that anger some time in the future. Juan prayed hard as he moved.

They came out on the other side of the river, dripping wet. Clothes, shoes, plastic bags soaked, water streaming from them as they left the river. They started walking at a steady but comfortable pace.

Juan giggled because his shoes were making squishing sounds, and Carlotta smiled at her dear little man child. Tío Juan. Her husband's little brother, whom she loved as her own.

"We are lucky to be safe and wet too," Carlotta commented. "We will be cool until we dry out."

Juan nodded. "Tell me about the convent, Carlotta."

"It is a very nice place, bigger than the one at home. It has a school and a clinic, and a place that sells things as well.

"La tienda!" Juan's eyes grew big, picturing it. "And you have written to them?"

"Yes, I have."

Carlotta was vaguely uneasy about not telling Juan everything. But one thing she could honestly assure him of. "They liked the shirt I made, the one Carlos had on when we visited there, and some of the things I showed them that I had sewed. Nothing is really settled yet. But we will see."

They walked a long way before their clothes and shoes dried, and both of them were tired. Plodding on, so bone weary the pace was automatic.

"Soon it will be light enough to see the map and we will look and see where we can stop to rest."

"It is on the map? Where Carlos stopped?"

"Yes, we will stop to rest and eat before we go on."

Juan nodded, trying to picture the convent and the store. Excitement dimmed the fear he felt. His legs and lungs were as weary as old men, but his hopes and imagination were still fourteen years old. He walked beside Carlotta, vowing to take care of her as he had promised Carlos.

CHAPTER TWO

The day was just beginning to heat up to the typical Las Flores temperatures and was still pleasant where there was any shade. But there wasn't much shade in the big market area where workers were gathered to find jobs.

A man standing in a sheltered place was talking to the people gathered in front of him. There were quite a few men standing or looking around in the big open space. A lot of them had stopped to listen. Carlos Castillo and his cousin, Jorge Brazos, paused to see what was getting so much attention.

Jorge looked toward the man who was speaking to them, trying to recruit workers. The gringo was a large, florid-faced man with the kind of smile seen on used car salesmen, New York ad men, or politicians.

The two of them sat down just inside the shelter's shade and listened till Jorge touched his cousin's arm. His face was excited.

"Think of it, Carlos! What he offers is double the money we are getting now!"

There was no answer from Carlos, and the man kept talking to the crowd.

Jorge again looked hopefully at Carlos, who remained silent through Jorge's argument as well as the good things the man was promising.

"Double our money! This is good, no?" Jorge pressed for an answer.

Carlos sighed and shrugged his shoulders. "I know only what he says. What he promises. It sounds good —" He stopped. Their talk was attracting attention of some of the others.

"Let us go outside, Jorge." Jorge dutifully followed his cousin out.

"He has much work for us to do, he says, and he owns a business." Jorge started as soon as Carlos stopped outside. His forehead wrinkled, looking puzzled. "Why is it you do not think this is good?"

The answer came plainly and without hesitation. "I do not trust the man, Jorge." Carlos shook his head. "He does not seem to me to be an *hombre* you can trust."

"I too wondered about why he must offer more money to get workers. I do not know why he comes to us with this offer. But he is not paying, even at double, what he would have to pay if he kept the gringo workers for the whole year. And he would have to pay other things to them, too, that he will not have to pay if he uses us. I don't know if we can trust him. But I trust that we can get more money from him if it is good for him."

Jorge's weathered, honest face took on a look as close to sly as he could get. "He has a business to think of. And if it is good for him it will be good for us, too, no?"

"You are right about that," Carlos admitted. "And no matter what he thinks of us, we have our papers. We can work where we choose and we will make the money we need. Maybe not double as he says, but we will have work."

Jorge looked toward the low building behind them. "But others are signing with him now. If we stay out here talking about the good salary too long, he will have all the men he needs," Jorge warned as he looked back.

Carlos looked back, too, at the building and the bus. "The money does sound good. We will go and speak to him — we will ask him one or two more things."

He started in the direction of the building

and Jorge followed, shaking his head and muttering half to himself. "One or two more things?"

Approaching the front of the crowd, Carlos and Jorge went back to the shelter and approached the crate that was serving as a desk for the man's paperwork. They stood waiting as the man spoke, his name pasted on a poster on the crate.

As the man stopped for a drink of water, Carlos said respectfully, "Mr. Mansfield?"

"Yes?" Mr. Mansfield turned toward them with a wide smile, taking in both of them. "Do you want to sign on to work?"

"I . . . we do not wish to sign any kind of a contract." Carlos said it doubtfully, looking down at the papers lying on the crate.

"But we do want to work," Jorge added quickly with a smile every bit as wide and phony as Mansfield's.

Mansfield chuckled. "This paper is no contract or anything like that. It's a list of who will be going. We have to know how many we have to go so I can call ahead and tell my office how many are coming. There is no contract."

"Is it very far to your place? And how will we be paid? My friend and I have not been here long. We only heard you telling the men that the pay is good."

They were treated to another one of Mansfield's wide smiles. "I see. Money sounded good to you, did it? Well, it is. The way you get paid here, by the weight you pick, is not even half of what you will make at my place. You will work set hours a day and be paid for them. And the work is not hard. We are making crates of all sizes. Wooden crates."

He saw the concern appear on Jorge's face. "But you don't have to be a carpenter. You will learn. Right now, I have a contract for overseas crates, the big ones. I'm sure you've seen them —"

"*Sí,*" Jorge said eagerly. Carlos nodded; both were picturing themselves putting together the big crates. Carlos thought it would be a good thing to learn more about carpentry, but his mind always returned to the money offered.

"And how will we be paid?" Carlos insisted.

Mansfield almost frowned but answered with as pleasant an expression as he could muster. "You will be paid by the week. In cash."

Jorge held his breath. Carlos still hesitated.

"And . . ." Mansfield smiled again. "You will stay in a barracks near the shop. A meal in the morning and a meal in the evening will be furnished to you. It won't be steak." He chuckled. "And of course you are free to go and eat elsewhere if you want to. But the two meals will be furnished if you want them, along with transportation up there."

"Transportation?" The doubt leaped from Jorge's face to Carlos like an infection in the heat of the place. They had only worked in Las Flores before this.

"Where is this place?" Carlos asked seriously, thinking over the little information Mansfield had given them.

"It's up north of here. Takes about three hours or a little more at most to get there." Mansfield's curt answer showed he was getting a little weary of all the questions.

He smiled broadly at Jorge, who was clearly the one more interested in his proposition. "If you and your friend are interested, just sign your names here and wait over there with the others. By my sign over there," he pointed.

Carlos finally nodded and both of them stepped closer to the crate desk to sign their names. Mansfield looked on, beaming his approval, and looked at the two signatures. It was done. They were signed in and they were going on the job.

"For a minute or two there, I thought we were not going," Jorge whispered as they turned away.

Carlos laughed at that and pointed to the far outside wall. They walked to it and put their backpacks down.

"Let us sit here where we can lean back. I did not see anyone we have worked with before and he did not ask to see our papers. He must have an order to fill for these crates and needs help quickly for him not to ask for our papers." Carlos looked around at the men waiting and the ones Mansfield was still talking with. "I wonder how long we will have to wait?"

"I do not know." Jorge looked at the men waiting. "There may not have been many we know at the place where we usually work either."

"But usually there are more questions."

Jorge studied his sandals, not meeting his friend's eyes. "It may be you were right to question him, Carlos."

"Fine time to start worrying," Carlos teased him. "Don't worry about it, Jorge. We have our papers and we are not slaves. If it is not as good as he says, we can leave and come back. Or there will be other work there. We will not have to stay if we don't want to. And we are together. Just keep your mind on going home, Jorge."

Oliver's sense of loss when he couldn't find the beautiful *señorita* surprised him. *Get a grip,* he scolded himself. *Besides, Las Flores is not very big. We'll probably meet again. And too, she could be married.* He quickly discarded that idea.

Oliver made his way back to buy his supplies, firmly shaking off the idea his dream girl might be someone else's dream and have a husband. He scowled down at the pile of supplies. Sometimes it looked to Oliver as if everyone in the world was married but him.

He shook the self-pity and added three or four more items to the jumbled pile. Glad he had his art and his job, he took his supplies to be checked.

The thought of his summer art class lightened Oliver's mood. He liked teaching, and it was a good group he had for this summer course. The class was a pretty mixed group, with some older people in it who were doing surprisingly well and obviously enjoying the course.

When he got everything in the car, he stopped by the store for steaks and a case of Cokes.

He knew his best friend, Matt, and Matt's girlfriend, Joanna, would already be at his house if Matt had decided to quit early. He wondered now why he'd suggested cooking out when they were going to treat him to a meal?

At the time Oliver had felt like cooking out, but the mood seemed to have melted in the heat. His mind went to Matt as he drove home.

He's been acting funny lately. I wonder if he's going to tell me he and Joanna are getting married?

When he turned the corner on his street, Oliver saw a small red convertible sitting in front of his house. Matt and Joanna were there. He smiled to himself. The door was open and Matt knew how to make himself at home. As he parked and started to get the groceries, Matt came out.

"Looks like you could use a little help there."

"Wouldn't hurt. You take these and I'll get the other sack. Where's Joanna?" He handed Matt the sack he held.

"She headed straight for the pool. It's great to have rich friends in weather like this!" Matt easily juggled the grocery sack in one hand and the case of Cokes in the other and headed into the house.

Oliver grinned with affection, watching him manage all that. "It's good to have a meathead coach for a friend too. I'd have had to make two trips."

Inside, he put the steaks in the sink and stuck his head out the back door to greet Joanna.

"Hi! Sorry to be late. Had to pick up a few things at the mall."

"No problem," came her cheery voice. "I'm enjoying the water. And swimming is better for you than eating anyway. Yell if you need some help!"

"I won't, but thanks." He turned to see Matt standing behind him with an affectionate grin on his face. It was a definite *I've Got News* face. Oliver braced himself for whatever the announcement was.

"Ollie, old pal," Matt started.

Oliver gave him a sideways glance as he prepared the steaks. "Things that start out that way usually wind up costing me money."

He'd had time to imagine several other things when Matt shook his head. "Not this time. Price of admission is free." Then he blurted it out, "Joanna and I are going to get married!"

"No kidding?" Oliver laughed at Matt's expression. "It's about time. That's great!

Congratulations." He wiped his hands and stuck one out.

Wordlessly, Matt bypassed the hand and gave him a bear hug, sighing with relief. "I didn't know how you'd take it. I'm glad you approve, *Dad!*"

"I may poison you, *Son,*" Oliver growled.

"Heck no, you won't! You'd have to send out for aggravation!"

Matt went out to wash the sand off the picnic table, which stayed where it was regardless of heat, sand, dust, or whatever winter threw at Las Flores. Oliver followed to put the steaks on the fire and wrapped up some potatoes to go with them. They had plenty of time to swim and cool off while their dinner cooked on the grill. And Oliver could get used to the idea of Matt being married.

Later, all of them full of steak and warm feelings, they sat at the picnic table and talked. Matt and Joanna's affection showed when they looked at each other. Oliver was happy for them in spite of feeling even more alone than usual.

"I'd about decided I'd have to propose for you, it was taking you so long," Oliver told Matt. He winked at Joanna. "Was it my hints that woke you up, or are you going to claim all the credit for the idea?"

"Well, Ollie," Matt shot a look at Joanna, who nodded slightly. "I guess it was a combination of your hints and my feelings, and one other little thing."

"Oh, and what was that?" Suspicion was instant. Oliver knew Matt's weakness for jokes.

"We both want a little Matt — or Joanna."

Oliver whooped, picturing a pint-sized Matt with a miniature baseball bat in his hand. Delighted at the idea, he took Joanna's hand in both of his. "Just don't let him talk you into having him a home-grown baseball team!" He laughed at Matt's indignation.

"Who asked you, killjoy?" Matt scowled.

Oliver slapped Matt's broad back. "Well, team or not, congratulations!"

"You know, Wisenheimer, it just might happen." Matt got a dreamy look on his rugged features before coming back down to earth. "But I proposed to Joanna before I knew twins run in her family. And besides, you're just jealous!" Looking smug, Matt took a swing at him

"Twins? You are lucky. And you got it right, I am jealous. I really am." He grinned at them. He glanced down at the Coke beside his plate. "If I'd known this was coming I'd have got more than Coke to toast the good news with."

"Coke is fine, Ollie," Joanna told him. "It's the thought that counts. I can just start now, not doing any social drinking until we get little Matt or Joanna's invitation sent." She giggled. "Bring on the vitamins!"

When they finished, Joanna insisted on washing the few dishes they had used so Matt and Oliver could sit outside and talk a little while. They talked about changes Matt was going to make in his small house until they could save enough for a larger one and about the baseball team Matt was getting together at the park.

Matt liked his job as coach at the local high school and was good at it. Oliver couldn't imagine him doing anything but coaching, though it wasn't as lucrative as some of the other things he knew Matt was qualified for.

"I wish teaching and coaching the kids at the park paid something," Oliver said thoughtfully.

"Tell me about it!" Matt agreed. "But it's fun for me and keeps the kids out of trouble. And along more practical lines, I know by working with them during the summer which ones can hit and pitch when they come to try and make the team at school."

"Yeah, I know that must be a big help

when you have to screen them and get the best ones you can."

It was a good visit, with the pool to cool off in, good food, and good company. Joanna fit right in and Oliver was happy for them. Matt and Joanna were exactly right for each other.

After Matt and Joanna left, Oliver smiled to himself, making sure everything had been put away. But putting things away didn't last long and the lonely quiet settled around Oliver like a distant echo of laughter in the silence.

Sitting there having a last Coke, Oliver thought about the bittersweet memories of good times he'd had with Matt, the fun they'd had together. Now that unpredictable rascal was getting married. He knew this was inevitable but it still reminded him how alone he was. Oliver thought of the beautiful girl he had seen at the mall.

She was searching the incoming crowd. Those eyes seemed to search every face. Maybe she's lonesome, too.

He shrugged away that idea. *No, not a chance, not someone as lovely as that.*

He got up and went inside, trying not to feel sorry for himself, certainly not begrudging Matt and Joanna their happiness.

Humming "Spanish Eyes" to himself, Oliver went to his studio and absently picked up a charcoal pencil. Without making any decision to work, hardly realizing what he had in mind, he began to sketch the face and eyes that were haunting him.

CHAPTER THREE

Sister Rosa hurried down the long, cool hallway. She had been summoned and wondered what the Mother Superior wanted.

When she knocked gently on the edge of the door, Mother Clare's face lit up with a welcoming smile.

"Come in." She held out a tiny dress to show her. It was long and white and beautiful, with tiny tucks and embroidery around the neck.

"This is a christening dress. Look at it and give me your opinion of the workmanship."

Sister Rosa took the delicate little garment and looked closely at it. She turned it inside out, examining the seams as well as the intricate embroidery done in pastel colors and other work on it. Then with a pleased expression she gave her opinion.

"It's one of the prettiest christening dresses I've ever seen. The work is excellent. The embroidery is beautiful as well."

"Those are my feelings, too. About this and the other two pieces that were sent to us with it." Mother Clare's smile faded. "But I'm afraid there may be a problem attached to them."

"A problem?" Sister Rosa was puzzled. "Who sent them to us? Do they ask too much?"

"No. No, it's not that. The young woman who sent these . . ." Mother Clare paused to push forward an opened brown paper package. "You may as well look at the others."

Sister Rosa handled the other two pieces carefully, looking critically at the work on them as she had the christening dress.

"If you remember, several months ago a young couple stopped to spend the night with us. The woman had on a scarf she had made and she had made the shirt her husband was wearing. It was his best, came by the clinic after mass. I happened to be there at the time. I saw the scarf and shirt she had made and complimented her on them."

"I remember your telling me about it, and about her asking you about working in the store or the clinic. It stuck in my mind since we are sometimes in need of help in the store. These are from her, then?"

"Yes, they are her work."

Sister Rosa smiled, looking relieved. "If you have already talked to her, what is the problem?"

"Nothing was decided then, although we could use some help now. What worries me is the reason they came to the clinic on their way home was that she had just been told she was with child, and they got some vitamins and things for her."

"I see. She would be well along now." Sister Rosa paused and silently counted the months. "But Mother, this is a blessing —"

"The problem is, there was a letter with these things. They came this morning and the young woman is on her way here. She should be arriving in the next day or two."

Mother Clare's worry lines deepened. "I am afraid she is coming — without the blessings of the United States government, to put it mildly."

Sister Rosa caught her breath. "But if she said she is coming, perhaps she has papers allowing her to come and work?"

Mother Clare turned a sad look on her. "No. When they came by here, she only had permission for two days, and she was traveling home with her husband who *does* have permission to work here. And neither of them said anything about her returning."

"There is something more, isn't there?" Sister Rosa felt it, reading her expression.

"Yes. I hope I am wrong, but I have the feeling she may be coming — to help us here as she said, yes. I believe she is sincere in that. But the main reason she is coming may well be that she wants her baby to be born in the United States."

Both of them sat silent, thinking of the visitor, her baby, and the possible consequences of her coming to the convent. It was not a bright picture.

"But the sewing is excellent, so there are good things to consider. Perhaps she will have permission, though she did not tell us she had. Let us pray about it and we will see what she has to say when she comes to us."

"I have already started my prayers for her." Mother Clare sighed and put the brown paper back around the beautiful little garments.

Eleana frowned at the phone. "Slowly, *slowly, por favor!* How can I understand you? *Raquel!*"

"I am sorry! I am sorry!" It was almost a sob. "It is just that I am so upset, Eleana!" The anguished feminine voice on the phone

45

apologized, and Raquel caught her breath.

"And I am sorry I yelled at you." Eleana's affection and concern could be heard in her voice. "Now, tell me. What has happened to upset you so?"

"I went over to Carlotta's, to take her and Juan some tomatoes from my garden. I didn't see them yesterday. I had so many things to do —"

"Of course you do. I know you do." Eleana tried to calm her, bringing her back to what was wrong. "You went over to Carlotta's, and?"

"When I got there the door was closed and locked. There was no one around. I called Juan, thinking Carlotta might have gone for a walk. She does this sometimes in the afternoon when it is not too hot."

"And the door was locked?" Eleana was puzzled too; Carlotta did not usually shut and lock the door unless she was going to be gone longer than the walks she took for her daily exercise. "Were the back doors locked as well? Perhaps she just forgot to unlock the front one —"

"Yes. They were locked too. And she and Juan, they are both gone. I waited for a while then decided I would come back the next morning. I felt they would surely be there then, in the morning."

"But they were still not there?" Eleana's brows drew together as she pictured their small house.

"No. I was worried and I looked in the windows and tried the back door and the low windows back there. But everywhere, everything is locked. The doors and all the windows were closed and locked." Raquel started to cry. She moaned, "It is as if they are *never* coming back!"

Eleana felt weak. *Gone?* She thought. *This is a frightening thing, and Carlotta is with child!* Aloud, she tried to sound reassuring and spoke softly to Raquel.

"Raquel, had Carlotta mentioned anything to you about going anywhere to visit? Or taking Juan fishing, like Carlos does sometimes? You know, he showed him how to build a lean-to —"

"No, nothing was said about a visit or camping or fishing, or anything like that. And they didn't tell me they would be going. I only went over there and found them gone. Oh, if only I had gone to see about Carlotta yesterday, maybe —"

"No, no. Do not blame yourself like that, Raquel. She had Juan with her, and you were nearby if she needed you. Think, Raquel, when was the last time you saw her? And was Juan with her?"

"I saw them coming back from church. Both of them. They waved to Paco and me. There didn't seem to be anything wrong."

"When you looked around the house, Raquel, everything seemed all right? Nothing had been broken or seemed out of place?"

"No, Eleana. It was just, as if they had gone somewhere to visit. And had closed and locked everything up."

"Well . . ." Eleana's voice rose with hope. "That is probably exactly what happened. They went somewhere visiting or fishing and they are together. Do not worry; they will probably be home soon."

At the other end of the phone line, she wiped the tears from her cheeks, wanting to believe in this visit. "Well, maybe you are right. When are you going to call me again, Eleana?"

"I will call you there at *la tienda* at this same time next week. Keep an eye on the house and watch for Carlotta and Juan, but do not worry, and I will call you then." Eleana did not mention that she had not found Carlos. Raquel was already upset. She sighed. "I'll call you next week."

"All right, Eleana . . ."

Eleana walked into the neat stucco office

building and tried to ignore all the attention she was getting from the men lounging and waiting for word of available work. She looked straight ahead, uncomfortable. She walked fast, as worried as she looked. She was dressed beautifully and properly, keeping her eyes in front of her and her worry and hopes to herself, in order to make a good impression on her brother's former employer. She needed his help to find Carlos.

There were three people in line in front of her to make inquiries about their people who were working where Carlos had said he would be. When her turn came, she asked where Mr. Lehandro's group was working.

"They will not be through working for another two hours or more." The clerk looked suspiciously at her.

"I do not wish to disturb them," Eleana explained earnestly. "I have a message from home for one of the men who is working for Mr. Lehandro. He has worked for him before. If you will tell me where they are, I will just tell him and leave." Eleana fastened her fast-dwindling hopes on the name of the man Carlos had given her. Mr. Lehandro.

"They are at Farrel's Grove today." Then deciding to be helpful, the clerk added, "It is a long hot way for a walk. Or even a ride on a horse. They will be back near here at the end of the day."

Eleana looked up, hope returning to her eyes.

The young man explained, "Farrel has rented a bunkhouse for them. I can give you the address of the bunkhouse if you want it."

"Mr. Lehandro will be there then as well?"

The clerk nodded.

"Yes, I would like to have it." Eleana took the hastily written address and thanked him, leaving through the sea of bold eyes, more confident now, moving quickly.

She followed the clerk's directions and walked to the bunkhouse so she would know where to go later, and waited till the end of what the clerk said was the workday.

When the time came, wearing her comfortable sandals, Eleana set out for the bunkhouse hoping that if Carlos was not there, she could at least find out where he had gone. She would talk to Mr. Lehandro himself.

The beginning of sunset was beautiful, the streetlights were already burning, and there were scents of supper cooking along the way. Good scents were coming from the bunkhouse, too, when she approached the door.

No one answered her knock. She tried again, knocking harder, anxious about her brother.

The harder knocking brought a laughing response, "Don't worry about getting in, pretty lady," some young male voice called to her. "The problem will be getting out!"

A rough-looking man came to answer her knock. His browned skin made his blue eyes startling in his weathered face as he grinned at her. He had heard his young employee's comment.

"What can we do for you, ma'am?"

"I would like, if I may, to speak to Mr. Lehandro."

The large man stood inside the door, not close enough to appear threatening, and he spoke politely. "I'm Lehandro."

Eleana took all this in and spoke respectfully. "I am Eleana Castillo. I am looking for Carlos Castillo. He is my brother, and he is working for you. Or I thought he was." She hesitated. "The clerk I spoke to when I called to ask about him was very nice, but said he is not here. But . . ." Her troubled eyes searched his face. "This is where he told me he would be."

"Yes," Lehandro nodded. "He's supposed

to be. He told me he was coming and I had work for him. But I guess he got an offer that sounded better to him. He's not here now."

"Not here? But, where did he go?"

"I'm not sure of that." Mr. Lehandro rubbed the back of his neck as if the muscles ached. "There are always people coming in to get workers and making them offers. I guess he must have gone with one of them. He just came and told me, since he knew I would be expecting him. He said he would probably work for me again, but he seemed to be in a hurry."

"He didn't say where he was going to work?"

"No." The man frowned a little, looking sympathetic. Eleana's worry showed on her pretty face. She simply stood silently, not knowing what to ask next.

"Look here, if you need some sort of help . . ." Lehandro started.

"Oh, no. No," Eleana managed a weak smile. "But thank you."

The startling blue eyes smiled but Lehandro seemed relieved he wouldn't be called on for help. He rubbed a hand across his forehead and Eleana noticed the gold wedding band on his finger.

"What about Jorge Brazos?" Eleana asked

hopefully. "Jorge is a friend of his, his cousin. They came here together. That is, they planned to come and work together."

"Yes, I remember Jorge. He was with him. Wherever they are, they must be together."

Eleana thanked him again then turned away. She walked back toward her rooming house, her mind puzzling over the little she had learned.

What could have made him and Jorge leave like that? He has worked for Mr. Lehandro for three seasons now. And what made Carlotta and Juan leave with no word to anyone? But Jorge must be with Carlos as Mr. Lehandro said. And Juan is with Carlotta, she thought, feeling a little better.

Suddenly she smiled to herself. *If Carlos has left the people he has worked with for three seasons, then he must have got a much better offer. That must be it, a chance to make more money.* It was comforting to believe they were making more money. That Carlos and Jorge were all right.

And they may still be working in this area. They probably are. I will look where there are lots of people. I will find Carlos. The mall is always full of people, he told me. So sooner or later, surely, if Carlos is still nearby he will come into the mall.

When Eleana went to the mall the first

time, she walked slowly and searched both floors. But there was no sign of Carlos or Jorge. She realized with a start after searching the lower floor that she had expected to see Carlos or Jorge. As if it would be that easy! She scolded herself and resolved to keep looking if she didn't hear from Carlos or Jorge soon.

I will go up to the second floor that faces the doors and watch the people who come in for a while before I leave.

She had stood there looking down, searching every face in the incoming crowd for Carlos or Jorge. There were lots of people there between work and the dinner hour.

One of the people in the crowd caught her eye. He was a handsome man, tall and with blond streaks in his hair. Eleana drew in a quick breath, not looking directly at the man. She studied him from the corner of her eye, looking back at the entrance. Her heart skipped a beat as she watched him. He had stopped for some reason, but she dared not look directly at him. He had come in alone, in casual dress. But as he passed under the skylight, the glint of gold in his hair and his strong features made Eleana's knees weaken so that she put her hand on the mezzanine rail in front of her.

A golden one, his hair is like the golden

brown bears in the summer. She sighed to herself, admiring his tall, fit body, still pretending not to see him.

Eleana kept her eyes moving, searching, so he wouldn't know she was looking at him.

I wonder who he is, if he lives here. I have not seen him at the church. But I cannot stand here daydreaming. I must go.

Eleana forced herself to turn away, to walk back down the aisle of shops one more time before going home.

No use to waste my time dreaming of the golden one. I must find Carlos. I must!

That night Eleana slept, but dreamed of endlessly searching crowds of faces for Carlos. There were cruel dreams, too, of Carlotta and Juan being swept away in the Rio Grande's swollen current in a storm or running from armed patrols along its banks. In and out of her dreams, the man with the golden glints in his hair appeared. Dreaming, fascinated, she studied every angle of the stranger's face with the strong bones and the frame of fair hair the skylight's beams had lit up with strands of gold.

CHAPTER FOUR

Juan and Carlotta continued walking, watching for patrols on the United States side of the river.

Mistaking Juan's silent concern for her and the child for tiredness and fear, Carlotta reassured him. "It isn't too much farther now, Juan, where we are going to stop and rest."

Juan nodded. He raised his eyes and looked ahead at the beginnings of a wood in the distance. The trees were just beginning to stand out against the approaching dawn.

They reached the first of the trees safely. At least now they were hidden by the thickening trees and underbrush. Juan felt safer, the tenseness between his shoulders relaxing a little.

"We can slow down some now, Juan. It is safer here among the trees, and we must watch for the place Carlos told me about."

"It is a cave? We do not know this place, Carlotta. How are we going to find a hidden cave?" Juan had not wanted to come. His fear was not as great as his guilt or as uncomfortable. He knew it was dangerous for them, especially for Carlotta. But he saw no other choice. He could not let her go across the river by herself.

I promised Carlos I would take care of her.

"There are landmarks we can look for." Carlotta's voice broke into his troubled thoughts. "There is one, there." She pointed.

"That is only a dead tree, Carlotta." Juan frowned.

"Yes. A big dead tree, and it is leaning on that smaller dead tree. As if someone placed it like that. It would have taken two grown men to place it like that, as Carlos told me. And listen, do you hear that?"

Juan listened. "Yes, it sounds like water."

"Yes, the water is over there to our right. The tree is straight ahead, and somewhere along here in a lot of undergrowth is the entrance to the cave." Both stopped talking, eyes searching carefully.

"Carlotta!" A few steps ahead, Juan called over his shoulder, "I think I have found it. But it looks small. Come and see if this is the one we are looking for." He stood waiting near some bushy undergrowth where a gust of wind had revealed a small opening.

Carlotta took the stick she carried to make sure of the opening. After a little exploring with the stick, she straightened up. "It must be. Carlos said it is not very big and there are the dead trees, propped together, and across from the water —"

"Wait." Juan let the brushy cover he was holding spring back. "I will take the stick and go in first since I am smaller than you. And there may be a snake or two in there."

"Take the stick then if you think there may be snakes. And as you look around see how far back the cave goes."

"Well," Juan said after a few more jabs and blows to the earth with the stick. "There are no snakes, I guess." He tossed away the stick. "I will call to you when I get in."

"Wait. Take the light, Juan."

He reached back for the light and disappeared into the hole, glad she couldn't know how afraid he was. He imagined a sleeping bear, since there were no snakes.

The light showed him an opening about seven feet long and surprisingly high at the center. He turned and called to her, "Push the bags in and then come on in. But be careful. The cave slopes down as you come in, but there is plenty of room."

Carlotta looked back as she crawled into the opening. "It's getting lighter now. I'm glad we got here to be hidden before it gets too light. I didn't know how much room there was, but when Carlos told me about it, there were four of them who stayed in here. Four grown men going to find work, so I knew there would be room for us."

"We are across the river several miles now. Must we still hide?"

"Yes, we must. We must be careful, even after we reach the convent, Juan. I applied for papers, but they told me it could be many months before I can get them. And besides that, we are traveling alone. We will be safer when we lie down to sleep if we are hidden."

"I am ready to rest," Juan said wearily.

They had not slept long when Carlotta wakened. She drew in a frightened breath. *Voices. I hear voices!* She held her breath. There were several men passing by their hiding place. Two of the voices sounded angry. She heard Juan's breathing close to her in the dark; he didn't wake. Her heart went out to the tired little boy, and she was glad he was sleeping so soundly.

The footsteps hurried by and the voices faded. Carlotta slept again, grateful they had been safely hidden. When they awoke, the sun was high in the sky. They felt refreshed and hungry.

They left their things in the cave and went outside to eat by the water. Carlotta's sharp eyes saw one or two depressions, which could have been footprints, but she didn't tell Juan about the men who had passed by. The men talked as if they were hurrying for some reason, traveling so fast there would be no danger of her and Juan catching up with them. She turned to Juan with a smile.

"I brought some beans to spread on our bread, and water will wash it down all right. We couldn't carry too much." She wished she had something better to feed him.

"We will eat and wash ourselves, then get started again." He was hungrier than he realized and ate the bread quickly. He nodded when Carlotta offered more bread, his mouth too full to answer.

"Do not eat so quickly, Juan." She smiled at him. "Also, I will try to arrange the sack a little better before we start. The reason I had you wear your oldest clothes and brought that old horse blanket was so we could throw them away in the morning. We will eat, wash ourselves, and dress in the clothes I brought. We don't want to look suspicious by carrying a lot of things."

"And it will be less for us to carry."

Juan's words were braver than his thoughts, but his hunger was assuaged. His mind was full of doubts about coming across the river. About Carlotta getting too tired. And, most frightening of all, about facing Carlos when he found out what they had done.

They finished eating in silence, each wrapped in his own thoughts and fears. Carlotta prayed for her precious baby to be safe and born at the clinic by the convent, in the United States.

Juan knew it was her baby Carlotta put above all things right now, and he was afraid. *She thinks only of the baby. She would have tried to come by herself if I had not agreed to come with her. I had to come, I had to.* He tried to think of pleasanter things to keep from being afraid. *I wonder what Carlos and Jorge are doing now?*

"Aha, see? See here, doubting one?"

It was payday and the men at the crate plant had lined up for their promised wages. Jorge was grinning from ear to ear, happily counting out the bills. He put them in his pocket, looking at Carlos, who was still counting his money.

"Yes, I see." Carlos echoed his little bark

of laughter, glad they had got what they were promised. "I see a week's pay is what I see. So far, so good, eh?"

Jorge shook his head at the cautious answer. "You are a hard fellow to convince. The work is not too hard and the money is good. Who cares if you would not, as they say, 'buy a used car from that fellow,' as long as he pays us our money? *Muy bueno,* no?"

"*Sí, muy bueno.* We will keep our minds on getting our money and going home. But there is a lie he told us, Jorge. Don't you remember what he said?"

"About what?" Jorge frowned, squinting at him.

"He said when he was telling us about the morning and evening meals that would be furnished, that we could eat some place else if we wanted to. But there is no other place. No other place to eat or to call our people or anything else. We are out here away from everything. If there is some place near enough to walk, I have not heard of it."

"I know." Jorge looked a little dejected at the reminder. "I remember he said that. Let us ask around among the others and see if they know a place we could walk to."

Carlos shook his head, his face grim. "If there is a place, they do not know of it, and would not want to go to it anyway."

Jorge lost the rest of his enthusiasm. "You have asked some of them?"

"I tried to talk to five or six of them at different times."

Carlos glanced around them; there was no one close enough to hear or who even appeared interested in their talk. "And this worries me too, Jorge. All the ones I talked to speak only a very few words of English and they want no contact at all with anyone else."

His dark brows drew together. "They are afraid. You can see the fear in their eyes." There was fear now in his eyes, too. He stopped a shiver that started along his spine. "I have a bad feeling about this place, Jorge."

Jorge began to look more and more worried as he listened and commented, as if speaking to himself.

"He — Mansfield — didn't ask us about our papers or anything when he hired us as the men did at the other places where we have worked." Carlos nodded, eyeing some men a little distance away.

But Jorge was a hopeful fellow and with his pocket full of money, he was a born optimist. He shrugged away the bad thoughts. "But we do have our papers. So as long as he is paying us, I will not worry.

Let us go and eat!"

The meal was served in a shed built into the side of the work place. The meal they were served consisted of boiled cabbage and some kind of stringy meat that was hard to chew. There was more of some kind of dressing than the meat, and Carlos could not tell what it was.

"Not too good, but at least it costs us nothing," Jorge pointed out.

A sigh preceded Carlos's answer as he regarded the plastic plate before him. "Not like my Carlotta's good meals, but we will be going home soon. I am glad Juan is staying with her. My fine, manly little brother." Carlos smiled proudly. "It is good for him to have some responsibility, no?"

The thought of home and of Juan staying with Carlotta brought a smile back to his face. Carlos took a couple of bites of the stringy meat, trying to chew it into something he could swallow to keep his strength up.

Another two weeks went by, and Mansfield came around personally and gave each man his money on payday. He promised again to fix the broken water line to the multiple showers beyond the shed. It had broken twice now. Carlos had already vowed to himself he would not come back here to work in such bad conditions and so far away from everything.

"I will not come here again," he said softly to Jorge. "I will go back and work for Mr. Lehandro. He is a good man, and it is better to be in Las Flores."

"But we are here now, Carlos, and the promised money is good. Double, as he promised us."

Jorge was trying to win Carlos over to his way of thinking in spite of conditions. Both of them were happily leaving the meager meal when the overseer came up to them. He was a large framed and portly man with a florid face that did not take kindly to the sun. He was called Parker.

"Mansfield said to tell all of you that he's sorry there's no place around here to go or to phone. But if you want to send mail, have it ready in the morning before work. It will be a dollar for stamps and gas for each letter, and it will be taken to the post office for you." He didn't wait for comments and went on to tell the rest of the men.

"Well, now at least we can send word where we are and tell our people we are all right." Carlos was relieved.

"But, a dollar?" Jorge was outraged. "Why so much?"

"They do have to buy stamps and send a

man to the post office. And there is the gas to buy as well, as he said," Carlos reasoned.

"I think I could do it more cheaply than that," Jorge insisted.

"Don't worry. We will write together. Both of us will write just one page and put it in the same envelope. I will pay the dollar, and Carlotta can send Juan to deliver your letter for you."

"*Amigo!* That is what we will do!" Jorge was back in high spirits, looking forward to writing home.

The next morning the men lined up with their envelopes and cards to mail. Cards were a dollar too. Parker put the letters into sacks then put the sacks into the back of the jeep. That first morning, there were two big canvas sacks of mail to take.

Mr. Parker, looking pleased with himself as he got in to drive the jeep, smiled out the window as he left. He even returned some of the waves he got from the men.

About an hour later the jeep crossed a bridge over a deep canyon halfway to the closest little town. Parker slowed and stopped the jeep. He quickly transferred the money he had collected to his billfold and put the two bags out beside the jeep on the bridge. Getting out unhurriedly, he picked the sacks up one at a time. He opened and emptied them into the canyon below. He shook them to make sure all the letters and cards were gone and threw the empty sacks into the back of the jeep behind the driver's seat. With a grin of triumph, he got back into the jeep and continued toward town to buy supplies for Mansfield and some recreation for himself.

The next payday the men lined up as usual and were waiting to be paid. Mansfield was a little later than he usually was, and everyone waited anxiously for him, straining their ears for the sound of his jeep.

Some of the men were beginning to murmur and ask each other what might be wrong when Mansfield's jeep arrived. Parker, this time, was driving for him. Those who had sat down got up and resumed their places in line.

Instead of getting out, Mansfield stood up in the open-topped jeep where he could see everybody, and spoke to the men. The dead silence made it easy to hear.

"Men, we were held up bringing in the payroll and I'm going to have to owe you part of your money until next payday when we can make arrangements to get some more money sent out here."

There were resentful mutterings from the men but Mansfield held up his hands. "I know you've worked and you expect your money. This was something we had no control over. If you will just trust me until we can get things arranged and money transferred. You will get your money. It may be two or three weeks —"

The muttering was louder and angrier now, and Mansfield held up his hands again. "When this happened, I went into town, and I'm going to pay you out of my own pocket until arrangements can be made at the home office and the money can get out here. Each of you will get half of his pay now and the other half when home office sends us the money."

There was still muttering but not as angry now, and Mansfield took a leather briefcase out of the jeep. Mansfield started giving out the money, Parker standing by like a guard. It was then Carlos and Jorge noticed the gun Parker wore and the shotgun in the back of the jeep. Neither spoke of it, waiting to get their money.

After all the men got their money, half of what they were due, Carlos and Jorge sat down in the shadow of the building to put up their money and talk until the evening meal was prepared.

"Humph! We are back where we started from on the wages, eh, Carlos?"

"Yes. This is a little less than we were getting where we were before." He faced Jorge, meeting his eyes. "Do you believe him? About the money? About the holdup?"

"I don't know. That assistant of his —" Jorge frowned. "He has a look like he has, as the gringo says, 'put one over on us.' He is one I would not believe. Mansfield at least smiles and tries to look like he is trustworthy. Parker looks like a prison guard from an American movie." He spat in the dust. "Not even a false-friend smile like Mansfield."

"Maybe that is why Mansfield looks so phony to me." Carlos leaned back against the building. "I wonder if he only promised us the double money to get us to come out to this place. Not many would have come if they had known it was so far out and away from everything. And the conditions here, they are worse than the other work places are offering, too."

"Have you talked to any more of the men?"

"No. Well, one or two." Carlos drew in a deep breath, as if talking about the others was unpleasant and made him tense and uncomfortable. "But they are a suspicious lot and do not want to talk, even in our home language. I know they are our countrymen. But some of them, I would not trust them any farther than Mansfield and that Parker, his assistant."

As they sat there in brooding silence, leaning against the building, it would have been hard to decide which one looked more depressed.

"It was I who wanted to come here to work for Mansfield." Jorge felt guilty and didn't look at Carlos. He glanced down, studying the sandy dirt between his feet until Carlos spoke.

"I know you are blaming yourself that we are here, Jorge. But I was the one who decided I should come. The money sounded good to me, too." He tilted his head toward some of the others who were resting in the shade. "And we are not the only ones. Look how many others came here."

He smiled as Jorge began looking a little happier. "We will keep our minds busy with other things. We will think about going home."

At Juan and Carlotta's next stopping place, Carlotta had finished washing and was rearranging things in their plastic sacks while Juan played and swam like a carefree otter. She kept an eye on him as he floated on his back, then turned to dive down and swim some more. It would be a long walk to their next stop.

Juan came out of the water dashing big, wet drops out of his hair and looking to see what Carlotta was doing.

"I spread the blanket out flatter so you can carry it over your shoulder like a serape, and there is room in my little sack now for our light and what we have left to eat tonight. I think that will help."

Juan pulled on his trousers, shoes, and shirt, then placed the plastic-wrapped blanket over his shoulder. He settled it as if testing it. "You are right, it is easier to carry." He felt refreshed and strong, ready to continue their journey, able to take care of Carlotta. He was fed and rested and refreshed by his swim. Brave Tío Juan smiled to himself.

"We are ready then. Let us go." Carlotta looked around as they left, as if putting it in her memory to tell Carlos about later. Juan tried not to think about Carlos as they started walking.

The walking was steady but easier on them now. They followed the winding water-way and were always near enough to get a drink or to wet their clothes to stay cool.

"The shade and the water make it easier walking. No wonder Carlos and his friends came this way."

"That was two or three years ago, Juan. They still walk this way sometimes. But now that they have their papers in order, they usually have the money now to take the bus." She looked around. "I believe, from looking at the map, this is another place where they stopped."

"This getting the papers, this takes a long time?"

"Sometimes it seems a very long time." Carlotta's smile faded a little. "I wanted to get papers, as we should, but when the clerk told me how long it will take, at least six months and probably longer, I could not wait that long."

"You want very much for the baby to be born in the United States?"

"Yes, I do, Juan. There is more work here. And more trees and shade." She added and laughed at his expression as he squinted up at the sun coming through the foliage above them.

They walked on, not talking so much now, concentrating on hurrying along. Their last stop was still near the water. It was a park, and there were picnic tables and places to build a fire. Juan was delighted to see a pier built out into the water.

"If you will build us a fire, Carlotta, I will

catch us a fish!"

"And how will you do that?" She was amused at his excitement.

"In my pocket, I have a little plastic, waterproof matchbox. And in it is fishing line and two hooks." He was already reaching for it, eyes searching the ground for a cricket or some other bait. He picked up a sturdy-looking little branch as he looked around.

"All right, I will gather some wood and make us a fire and you will catch us a fish. But we still have our bread and beans if there are no fish."

"There will be fish." Juan went out on the pier and sat dangling his feet in the water, choosing a hook.

Carlotta looked in all directions, glad there was no one else there. The little park was not very far from Las Flores. She had been afraid there would be people. And people ask questions.

She had the fire started and had found a stick for the fish if Juan caught one. She got the blanket out of the plastic sack and took the clothes out that were folded in it. She shook them and decided they would look all right, not too wrinkled.

"Carlotta! I've got a big one!" Juan ran to her holding up the line and a large fish.

"Here, take him, and I will get us another one. There are more, I can see them!"

"This is a feast, Juan!"

Delighted, Carlotta got a knife from the sack with the bread and other food and started preparing the fish. She had the fish filleted and ready on the stick, and the other stick sharpened, when he brought her another fish almost as large.

"Two fat sun perch! You are a good fisherman, Juan. Put up your hooks now. This is a good meal for us. We will have fish and beans and bread."

"It is a good dinner, no?" Juan beamed as he put up his line and hooks.

"Yes, a good dinner. It will take a little while for them to cook. Why don't you have a swim, but don't go too far from the pier," she warned.

He nodded and shed his shirt and pants along the pier, running to the water.

That night Carlotta spread their blanket well back behind some bushes in case someone did come along, and they slept well. They would get to the convent the next day.

Both of them woke about dawn, excited at being so near their journey's end. They ate the bread they had left and carefully dressed in the clothes Carlotta had brought with them. The blanket and old clothes they folded and left under a picnic table.

"Maybe someone will find them who can use them. If not, it is a small thing for them to throw them in the waste can."

Carlotta had brought the one maternity dress she had bought and her best low-heeled shoes.

"You look nice, Carlotta," Juan told her as she straightened up.

"So do you, Juan. And we are ready. We will be there in about an hour."

"About an hour?" Juan's eyes shone with excitement. He walked, matching his pace to hers, stealing glances at her to see that she didn't look too tired and needed to rest. They spoke little until Carlotta touched his arm, looking excited.

"See those buildings up ahead, Juan?" Carlotta pointed to a distant steeple and the top of a roof that could be seen on the other side of a rise in the distance.

"I see it, I see it! Is it the convent, Carlotta? I see a cross! It must be the convent!"

"Yes, and as we get closer, you can see the other buildings. The cloister, the store, and the clinic. The clinic is not very big, but it is nice, and they are helpful to very many people. They are important to us right now, and they always need help in the store. That is what they told me when Carlos and I were here."

Juan nodded thoughtfully at what they could see of the buildings without commenting. He was not nearly as sure as Carlotta seemed to be that she would be able to find work there. He tried not to think of Carlos.

When they arrived, they went into the store first and looked around, then rested on a stone bench outside. Carlotta had wet her scarf in the restroom and now she pressed it to Juan's forehead and hers to cool them off.

"Now, I will go and ask to see the Mother Superior. Come, Juan."

She rose, showing much more confidence than she was feeling, and led the way to the convent's door.

Inside, she was told, by a very efficient-looking nun wearing glasses, that Mother Superior would not be in her office for two hours yet, but she would be glad to help her if she could.

"I — I wrote the Mother Superior a letter and sent some of the things I have made. To show her the quality of my work." Carlotta spoke slowly and carefully in English. "I am interested in working in the store and in making whatever is needed, and sewing, and, being whatever help I can be . . ."

Carlotta's voice trailed off, and she looked imploringly at the quiet figure of authority before her.

"I see." Sister Rosa nodded.

So this is the talented one who made those exquisite stitches. She is so young. And full of hope.

Sister Rosa's eyes were compassionate as she gave a slight nod. Aloud, she said as she rose, "Come into my office and we will talk where we can be comfortable."

Carlotta and Juan followed obediently and exchanged hopeful looks behind the narrow black habit.

In the office, Sister Rosa indicated chairs and sat down at her small desk, taking out a pad to write on.

She smiled kindly at Carlotta and took down the answers to her questions.

"Carlotta Castillo." She looked at the papers before her. "Yes, we did receive the things you sent. The work was very good." She looked up with a reassuring glance at Carlotta.

Juan was sitting close enough to give Carlotta's hand a pat of encouragement, which did not go unnoticed by Sister Rosa. She hid her amused expression by looking down at the papers. She continued asking questions and talking to them until she had all the information, both official by Carlotta's answers, and unofficial by her own observation. She did not ask where they lived or if they had any papers or permits.

"I will tell the Mother Superior that you are here to see her as soon as she comes in. It will be about two hours, and I will call you." She smiled at Juan. "You may wait where you came in, or walk around the store or the patio to pass the time if you want to."

"Thank you, Sister." Carlotta left full of hope, holding Juan's hand.

Outside, Juan spoke softly, "What do you think, Carlotta?"

"I don't know, Juan. They got the things I sent and she said they liked them. She did not tell us anything. She only got the information she thought they would need from me." Juan didn't comment but remembered the kindness of Sister Rosa's face.

Carlotta shook her head, "I don't know, but I am hopeful."

"Let us go to the store for a little while." Juan tugged at Carlotta's hand. "She said it would be two hours. Please?"

"All right. It will make the time go faster, as Sister Rosa said. But, we will not stay very long."

"All right." He quickly agreed and hurried to the door before Carlotta could change her mind.

The store was large and light, with glass all across the front of it. It was stocked with all sorts of what Carlotta called *turista* things, as well as skirts, scarves, dresses, and other clothes.

There was no one in the store but them that they could see when they came through the opening that connected it to the waiting area. Then the bell on the front door jingled and a heavyset Indian woman came from somewhere in the back.

Carlotta and Juan could hear her talking with a customer but paid no attention until the customer's voice rose in irritation.

"You mean there's nowhere I can get this skirt hemmed up? Really, as many people as come in here, you'd think there would be someone. Or someone you could recommend —"

To Juan's horror, Carlotta spoke up timidly. "I would be glad to hem it up for you, *señora.*"

All eyes turned on Carlotta, who now stood looking frightened at having spoken.

"How much?" the woman asked of Carlotta.

Carlotta turned scared eyes on the Indian

woman. Every inch of her silently cried for help.

The Indian woman's stoic expression did not change, but she spoke. "Narrow skirt — three dollar." It was a plain answer and had the ring of authority to it. The customer's expression relaxed.

"Three dollars is fine. When can you do it?" The last was addressed to Carlotta.

"I will do it now. Is there — where are the fitting rooms, please?" Carlotta's hand closed on her sewing kit in one of the deep pockets of her skirt.

The Indian woman pointed toward the back. The woman with the skirt in her hand was already headed that way as the Indian woman went toward the back door where she had entered.

Left alone, Juan waited. He wandered around the store, keeping an eye on the door where Carlotta had disappeared with the customer.

When the Indian woman returned, he helped her fold up some scarves she had brought from the back. He watched her first, then folded them as she did, both of them working in silence.

Finally, the customer came out of the fitting room. She was obviously pleased with her skirt and the service. She smiled at

Carlotta, who followed her.

"And will you be here now, to sew and make alterations that are needed?"

"I hope so." Carlotta smiled, clutching the three one-dollar bills. "Here or at the clinic."

The woman left, and Carlotta and Juan looked wonderingly at the three American dollars, forgetting about the Indian woman until she spoke.

"You will work here now?"

"I don't know. We, I am waiting to see the Mother Superior about working here or at the clinic. Anywhere I can that they may need help." Nervous, a little frightened at what she had done, Carlotta didn't know what else to say.

The Indian woman nodded, understanding more than they had told her.

"Let us go back, Juan, in case the Mother Superior comes to her office early. I want to make a good impression."

"No problem." Juan giggled happily. "You can tell her you are already working."

"No! No, I will say nothing. I will do whatever she says. I will work in the clinic or the store, or at whatever I can get."

CHAPTER FIVE

Payday came again for Carlos and Jorge and again, they got only half the salary that had been promised them.

"Another payday," Jorge spat out the words. "Half money and half promises!"

"Well, we are here now. We have no way to get back, even if they would take us back at Farrel's Grove. And the pay is a dollar or two more than we were making," Carlos wearily reminded him of their situation.

"But they *promised* us twice this much. That is how he got all these men to come here. I know you are right. But I feel like he tricked us into coming out here so far away that it is not easy to get back. It was part of his plan. He is as bad an *hombre* as you thought he was."

"At least we have written to let our people know that we are all right and where we are, as far as we know. He did not tell us the name of the nearest city. But it is only three more weeks now until we can go home to them," Carlos reminded him.

"I wish there was a mall where we could go and have a lemonade or punch and sit in the cool and watch the people. It would be pleasant." This came out wistful, almost a whine, as he remembered Las Flores. "There is nothing here, nothing." Jorge went on complaining until Carlos agreed with him.

"No, there is nothing else here. Even managing to get a shower is something to look forward to here. If we were near Las Flores, we could go to the mall every night there. My sister, Eleana, is working there now. In Las Flores."

"She already has her papers?"

"Yes. She was coming and she may be at the mall now, if she is through with her work."

"Lucky Eleana," Jorge grumbled.

Eleana was at the mall. She was again looking in vain for Carlos. She stood gazing down from the mezzanine, searching each face that came through the archway from the doors as she always did.

Suddenly she froze, eyes widening. *The Handsome One, he is here again! And he is looking at me! No, no. He cannot be, he does not know me.* Her eyes followed Oliver as he moved.

He was looking at me, he was. He is coming up the stairs!

Eleana turned and hurried down to the end of the passageway. She darted into the lingerie shop, not once looking back.

Not this time. You won't get away from me this time! Oliver set his jaw and took the stairs two at a time, keeping the long dark hair in sight. He smiled to himself as she went into the lingerie shop. Mere lingerie was not going to stop him. His heart beat fast from more than the rapid climb up the stairs.

As Oliver went in, two women turned a surprised expression on him. He ignored them. He was close enough now to reach out and touch Eleana.

"Please?" He touched Eleana's arm, an unaccustomed thrill going through his arm like an electric current.

She turned just enough to look up and see who it was who had touched her. When she saw him, Eleana shrank back against the counter, at a loss for what to say at such boldness. She simply stared up at him, unable to speak.

Suddenly speechless himself, his throat dry, Oliver swallowed and smiled down at the pretty face to gain time.

"I — I saw you when I was here before. A few days ago. You seemed to be looking for someone, as you were just now. Could I possibly be of help to you?"

If it had been anyone but the Handsome One, the Golden One, who offered help, Eleana would have been glad to accept, not struck dumb like a school child. But her thoughts were whirling, as confused as her emotions.

She tried to look pleasant and unconcerned. At least not as excited as she felt. Her heart pounded against her ribs and she tried to catch her breath and appear unaffected. It didn't work.

Oliver mistook her startled expression for worry and the fact that he was a stranger approaching her. She looked so frightened. He was afraid she would turn around and run.

"I was looking for my brother," Eleana said after a little pause and taking a deep breath. "But I did not see him." The last part came out sadly, without her realizing it.

"Your brother. You don't know where he is?" Oliver didn't understand the problem. As he tried to figure out how he could help, he realized his hands in his pocket were clenched into nervous fists.

I want to put my arms around her, feel her close to me. Umm, she smells good, or is it the potpourri and scents in here?

Their conversation was slow. Oliver and Eleana stood there, fascinated with each other, each trying to hide the anxiety the attraction between them was causing.

"A brother is a big item to lose." Oliver smiled, just glad to be in her presence. "How is it that you don't know where your brother is?"

Eleana shook herself from her frozen fear, but was still very conscious of how close he stood.

"Carlos. My brother's name is Carlos. He came here before I did. He is working somewhere in Las Flores. But he . . . I don't know where he is working," she explained.

"Oh, I see." Oliver looked puzzled a moment because he really didn't see, and he was trying to think of something helpful to say or do. "I have a friend whose brother will be able to help you. Matt is a good friend I've known for years and his brother, the sheriff here in Las Flores, can help you, I'm sure. It's part of his job to help people who live here and are here to work." Oliver talked quickly, trying to reassure her. "He could find out for you, where your brother is working. If you'd like me to, I'll talk to my friend and see what he can do."

Eleana didn't answer, as she thought about the possibility of getting assistance with her search. But her expression was still more frightened than hopeful.

After a brief gathering of courage, Oliver flashed a smile so torn by uncertainty it looked more like a leer. "Could we talk about it over dinner?"

She didn't answer, and the surprised expression on Eleana's face reminded him she was from another, more formal, culture where men did not approach women unless invited to do so. Oliver struggled to remember some of the things he knew of their culture from the time he had visited some friends who were painting in Mexico. He tried to recall the time he'd spent there, the people he had met. He started again.

"I'm — my name is Oliver Avery and I'm teaching art at Las Flores College. I live here, and I would like to help you."

"But . . . but . . ." Eleana hesitated. "I do not know you, Mr. Avery. My name is Eleana Castillo."

Oliver took her hand and shook it, grinning. "Well, now we know each other. Will you have dinner with me? I will ask my friend if his brother, the sheriff, can help you find your brother."

"It is kind of you to offer your help. But," Eleana said sadly, obviously wishing it were not so, "it would not be proper. I am sorry." The words sounded final as a marble slab. Oliver suffered, mind working on that, determined not to give up.

"Proper . . ." Oliver fished for an argument for *not proper. "To make it proper I will not ask you where you live so I can come and pick you up, although I would like to,"* he quickly added. *Pausing, his eyes came to rest on her face and he wanted to kiss her. She simply looked back in silence, as if there was no solution to the not-proper barrier between them.*

"We can meet here at the mall and have dinner at one of the restaurants here, all of us, not just the two of us. You and me, I mean. And my friend and his bride-to-be will be there to chaperone us. That will make it proper. And we can talk about how to find your brother for you."

"I . . . I don't know."

Oliver's heart leaped at the hesitation, his eyes holding hers in a silent plea.

Eleana wanted to see him again, to get to know him.

Afterward she was never really sure whether it was that, or her need to find

Carlos, that made her agree to meet him and his friends. *At the mall,* she reminded herself. *With chaperones, so it will be proper.* Her built-in conscience struggled with desire.

She did want their help. And he, the Handsome One, he had such nice and kindly eyes, as if he did want to help. *They have golden glints in them, like his hair.*

Talking amid the in-and-out, sometimes amused, traffic of the lingerie shop, Oliver and Eleana set an agreeable time to meet in the mall for dinner. As they parted, Eleana smiled at him, finishing the spell of enchantment that had started the first time he saw her looking down at him.

"All right, we will see you then. And we will see you safely home. All of us together," he quickly reassured her. Oliver was being careful to do everything right, respectfully and properly, and not frighten Eleana away.

He looked self-consciously around the lingerie shop. "I guess I'd better get out of here. I'm making the other customers nervous." He grinned back at two teenagers who were giggling at him. "I'll . . . we'll help you find your brother. See you here tonight!"

Oliver left quickly before Eleana could find any more objections or change her mind. He took the escalator back down to the lower level, his mind racing faster than his feet.

I've got to find Matt. He'll come if I have to club and drag him. He grinned to himself. *Joanna will help me when she finds out it's for a good cause.*

Matt was easy to find, but not easy to convince.

"*What?* Let me get this straight," Matt bellowed in his ballpark roar. "You picked up some babe in the mall and now you need an escort to take her to dinner? Give me a *break!*" Matt doubled over with laughter.

"Sit down, you clown, if you haven't wet your pants. I'll tell you about it."

Still chuckling, his face red, still muttering about how desperate "not proper" Ollie must be, Matt managed to sit down and shut up long enough for Oliver to talk to him.

"When you called and said we needed to talk, I would never in a million years have thought of something like this." Shaking his head, Matt cackled again with glee. "A *chaperone* yet." He rolled his eyes, "And you picked her up at the mall!"

"Okay, okay, simmer down. While you get hold of yourself, I'll go get something I want to show you."

Oliver left and came back carrying the charcoal drawing he had brought with him. The one he had done of Eleana. Wordlessly, he held it out for Matt to look at.

Matt stopped chuckling and took the drawing. His eyes on the sketch, he gave a low whistle. "Is this — But, I thought you said you didn't know her?"

"I didn't. I saw her at the mall about two weeks ago, and I've been watching for her around Las Flores ever since, trying to find her. Then today I saw her again. And this time I caught up with her."

"Caught up with her, hmm? Yeah. I definitely think you should tell me about this. Don't leave out anything." His eyes gave Oliver a piercing look. "If she's here 'looking for her brother,' there may be a problem here you shouldn't get involved in."

"What? I'm not asking for advice, *Mom,* I'm asking for *help.*"

"All right, all right. Tell me how come the pretty lady can't find her brother."

When Oliver finished telling Matt all he knew, he realized it wasn't very much. He answered the questions that followed without quibbling about them.

Matt asked if the brother had a permit to work, permit for permanent residency, or any other kind of papers. "Or just what is

91

he doing in Las Flores? Or did you even ask?"

"No, I didn't ask. We'll find out tonight. We'll have to ask questions about her brother to find him, so we can ask anything you think your brother, the INS or anybody else will need to know then."

It was clear Oliver didn't consider lack of information a problem. That didn't help Matt's peace of mind any. He almost winced when Oliver added, "We'll just ask her when she gets there."

"You mean, if she gets there." Matt was skeptical about the whole story. "You were pretty aggressive there, and she didn't tell you where she lives or anything else but her name."

"I was just glad I finally found her."

"Has *she* got any papers?" Matt narrowed his eyes at his friend, who still seemed to be floating about two feet off the floor.

"I don't know. Didn't ask. She won't need any if I marry her."

"*Marry* her? My *God!*" Matt cradled his head in his hands. "I've got to call Joanna."

"Oh, you're going to tell her what little you know and everything you suspect," Oliver growled. "So she can help you worry and give me a lot of good advice, too?"

"No." Matt finally had compassion for his

friend. "We'll tell her just enough to get her to the restaurant. And you're right about one thing. With the four of us, it will look a lot more proper." He shot a look at Oliver. "And if she doesn't show up, there's no sense in wasting an evening. We'll enjoy dinner together."

"Yeah, right. You would think of that."

"Joanna's giving me lessons in being practical, and other such useful crap as that." Matt grinned. "I knew you'd be impressed."

Joanna was pleased and excited about going to dinner to meet the mysterious woman, and hoping almost as much as Oliver that Eleana would show up. Matt told her more than he had planned. He was no match for Joanna's suspicions and woman's intuition.

"Hey, it's like a real-life soap."

On the way into the mall, Joanna teased Oliver. "Maybe this will be the special one. We've got to get you married, Oliver. I'm tired of you going around so happy and carefree." Matt and Oliver laughed with her.

At the mall they sat outside the restaurant to wait for Eleana. Oliver and Joanna were hoping Eleana would come. Matt was still undecided exactly what he should hope for.

Then Joanna touched Matt's hand beside

her on the wooden bench and Matt looked at Oliver.

Oliver was staring down the mall, his heart in his eyes. There was no mistaking that look. Matt groaned inwardly. Good, bad, or indifferent, Ollie was a goner.

"I guess she must be coming," he whispered to Joanna as he tore his eyes from not-proper Oliver's stricken expression to look for himself.

Oliver got up and stood waiting for Eleana, and Matt stared.

Joanna stared at Matt as he stared at Eleana. "Maybe I'd better take you home." Joanna took hold of Matt's arm as they got up.

Matt put his arm around her shoulders. "Not to worry, you've already landed me," he whispered without looking at her.

They stood beside Oliver to meet Eleana. Oliver introduced everyone and they started into the restaurant.

Eleana seemed a little shy but was, after all, among strangers, coping with a strange place and a strange language. All of them did their best to put her at her ease.

They refused drinks and as they waited to order dinner, Matt brought up the subject that had supposedly brought them there.

"Oliver tells me you are trying to find your

brother, Eleana."

"Yes," Eleana was relieved he had brought up the topic. "He is working somewhere here in Las Flores. He told me he would be here, but I don't know where he is."

There was a pause and Eleana said, "He has the proper papers. He has come here several years to work. And he told us, our family, where he would be working. He knew I was coming, that I would be working here too."

All of them were listening closely, and Eleana continued. "But I went to the place he was supposed to be, and they — the man who was in charge — told me he is not there."

"Oh, he *was* working there?" *Not hurt, killed, or disappeared suddenly,* Matt noted. "He had been working, but he left?" Matt thought of questions he knew his brother, Luke, would ask, and Eleana nodded.

"Where was that, where he was working? And who did you speak with?"

"It was . . . at least, the work was at Farrel's Grove. Carlos has worked there before, for the same man. And the man I spoke to, his name is Mr. Lehandro."

Oliver nodded and asked, "Did he, this Mr. Lehandro, say where he might have gone? And was your brother alone?"

"No," Eleana said slowly, thinking back to their conversation. "He didn't. He said that there were people from time to time that came into town and tried to get people to come and work for them, and he may have gone with one of them. He said Carlos — my brother's name is Carlos Castillo. He said that Carlos and his cousin, Jorge —" She raised her eyes to Matt's as she explained. "Jorge Brazos, was with him, but they had both left. He said they came and got their things they had left there at his place, thinking they would sign up to work there. But they did not stay to sign up to work again, as they had before when they had worked for him at Farrel's Grove. He does not know where they have gone. Before I went to talk to him, I had called the number Carlos had given me to ask about him. The woman who answered was very nice. But she did not find his name on her records. That is why I went to see Mr. Lehandro myself. I could not believe he was not there when he had given me the number and he had worked there before." Her worry showed as she repeated, "Carlos had told us he and Jorge were going to work for Mr. Lehandro."

"I'm sure it's a good thing there is someone with him," Joanna said with sympathy into the silence that followed. All of them were wondering what could have made Carlos change his plans.

"Yes." Eleana's Spanish eyes smiled at Joanna. "That is a comfort to me. But —" she sighed. "I do not know where they went. I don't know how to find him."

The waiter came then and took their orders and they waited until he gave them napkins and water and left them alone again. All eyes watched him as if he were some kind of entertainment provided by the restaurant, their minds busy on Carlos and Jorge's whereabouts.

Matt felt sympathy for Eleana as well as concern for Oliver. Along with knowing Oliver was about as smitten as one of his school team with a case of puppy love, Matt had a gut feeling — and it was bad. From what Eleana had told them, he felt certain Carlos was not one to simply disappear without telling his family.

"My brother is the sheriff here, and he takes his work very seriously." Matt smiled at Eleana. "I don't know what any of their Mickey Mouse titles are or much about what goes on down there, to tell the truth." Matt grinned, trying to lift Eleana's spirits. "But they all work together, and he will find out where your brother is for you. I'll tell

Luke about this, and I'll bet you couldn't keep him from making sure he's all right if you tried," Matt volunteered with the greatest of confidence. "It may take a little while," he warned. "Your brother's name's Carlos Castillo?"

"Yes. And his cousin's name is Jorge Brazos."

Oliver's face glowed with confidence in his friend, and Matt was so confident that Eleana smiled back at him, feeling better.

"Here's our food." Oliver reached over to pour more water in Matt's glass.

Eleana's heart beat faster just being seated next to Oliver. *My Handsome One. He and his friends, they will help me.* She watched as he poured his friend's water, thinking he was as thoughtful as he was handsome.

Joanna and Matt sat there reading Eleana and Oliver like two open books and exchanged knowing glances. Matt still had reservations. Some aspects of this situation looked serious enough to worry about. More questions needed to be asked, and he would keep an eye on Oliver.

CHAPTER SIX

Sister Rosa was waiting and got up when the Mother Superior entered her office.

"What is it?" she asked. "You look so concerned." She peered over her glasses at Sister Rosa.

"The guests we were expecting are here and waiting to see you."

"Oh, the one who does the sewing, who wrote to us?" She sat down and folded her hands on the desk in front of her, remembering Carlotta's letter. "You have talked with her? You said guests?" She looked up, her eyebrows raised. "Perhaps a little one?"

"Yes. Carlotta, who wrote us the letter. I believe she is about six months along in her pregnancy, perhaps closer to seven. But the other one, there is a young boy with her. About thirteen or fourteen, I'd guess. Or maybe older."

"Possibly a younger brother? I think she said in her letter he is her husband's brother.

And what did she tell you, and what is your opinion of her and the situation she is in? Did she mention having any papers or tell you where she is from?"

"I will start at the beginning and tell you all I could gather from the few minutes I talked to her."

"I was hoping she would say she had papers when she came. We do need someone in the store who can sew. And the clinic is always in need of help. But tell me what you have found out." Mother Clare listened carefully as Sister Rosa began.

"The first thing that struck me is how clean and cool they both looked. If they came to us as so many others have, by crossing the river and walking, they must surely have stopped somewhere to change clothes and wash themselves."

"That's good. It shows good sense and respect." Mother Clare nodded, favorably impressed.

"Then when I talked with Carlotta, I found she is indeed both intelligent and respectful, and, as I said, about six or seven months along in her pregnancy. She is small, so she may be even farther along. It is hard to tell sometimes. She was very anxious to make a good impression, and her eyes told me she is desperate for a job and a place to stay. She forgot to introduce me to the boy, and she showed her nervousness in other ways as well. I found myself really wanting to help them."

Sister Rosa's concern deepened as she pictured them. "The boy seemed very attentive to her and is well mannered. Had I the authority, I would probably give her a job and a place for them to stay, certainly, after seeing the kind of work she can do."

Mother Clare sighed. "Yes, I know how you feel. But it is such a problem, the having to have permission to work. It could cause problems for the convent if she were found to be here illegally." After a few seconds she fixed an intense look on Sister Rosa. "Do you think they are? Here illegally?"

Sister Rosa sat back in her chair. She looked like a flower wilting, and her face was sad. "Yes, I think they are, Mother. Anyone who has the proper papers is always anxious to show them to you. It is no doubt as you thought. She has come here so her child can be born in the United States."

Both of them sat trying to think of some way to help Carlotta that would not cause problems for the convent.

"Sister Rosa!" Mother Clare suddenly raised her head, a light in her eyes. "Go and get Stanley Jordan from the clinic. Tell him I need to see him as soon as he can get here."

Puzzled but full of hope that Mother Clare seemed to have thought of some sort of plan, Sister Rosa nodded and rose quickly. "Yes, Mother." She left, hurrying toward the clinic. Her black habit flapped around her thin legs, and she looked like some tall, thin, bird about to take flight.

Mother Clare smiled after her affectionately. *Rosa has the tenacity of a bulldog, which is a definite asset to the convent and me. She will bring Stanley no matter what kind of excuses he makes.* Her face relaxed into merry lines as she chuckled to herself.

It didn't take Sister Rosa long to find Stanley Jordan and summon him in no uncertain terms.

"Mother Clare?" He winced at the interruption. "I'm up to my eyebrows here, can't you see that?"

But Sister Rosa would not be put off. Stanley finally got tired of walking around her and went with her, reminding her in an insistent voice, "I must get back as quickly as I can!" He repeated that as soon as he got into the Mother Superior's office.

"Oh, is there some sort of epidemic we haven't heard about?" Mother Clare inquired innocently of the busy man.

Stanley fluttered around, finally standing in front of her desk to look down at her. "Yes, there certainly is! It's called a plague of shorthandedness, and we have it more often than not. We are even more short-handed than usual. I haven't had time to count the number of hats I'm wearing today besides business manager. Nurse's aide, maid, linen supply, receptionist, and on and on —" He looked so harried, Sister Rosa felt sorry for him, guilty about dragging him away from so many important tasks.

He related physical as well as stressful effects to Mother Clare, adding that was only a few of the problems facing him, till he was forced to stop for breath.

"I have a problem, too," Mother Clare told him. "And I think we may be able to help each other with our problems. Sit down," she commanded, waving him to a chair.

Struck by her positive attitude, Stanley Jordan sat.

"When you hire someone, do you ask all of them if they have permission to work here in the States? Or how do you handle that? And how do you handle the paying of temporary help? I do have a good reason for asking."

"The only reason we ask if they have papers is if someone comes to us who can't speak much English, and has an address in Mexico, or no address here. That makes it pretty clear you need to ask.

"One Indian man, a young brave, came and worked once just until he had enough cash in hand to buy a horse he wanted. He was a good worker, and we needed him. I thought he liked it here. But nothing could persuade him to stay. In spite of all our offers and pointing out he was needed and could have made more money for himself, he bought his horse and rode off." Stanley shrugged and shook his head.

This brought chuckles from the ladies, and Mother Clare lowered her voice so that Stanley had to lean closer to hear her.

"Stanley, we always have extra places for people who need them, and I am going to give someone a place to stay here. She and a younger brother. So their address will be the street address of the convent. She will be a guest, not an employee, so I will not ask anything about papers. However, if you need help, she might wish to come and apply at the clinic for work . . ." She looked hopefully at Stanley, waiting for what she had said to generate the ideas she was trying to get across to him.

"Hmm, I see," he said slowly, considering the unasked questions. "I am desperate for help, as you know. I need them right now. The lady and the boy. Could the boy pass for sixteen years old? But then, his mother or guardian is with him, and we could use him the limited number of hours for children." He raised his eyes to Mother Clare's. "But if he looks sixteen and wants to work, I will not ask or need permission from his mother or anyone else. These things are looked at more closely than other hiring practices because they involve children. But what do you think? Could he pass for sixteen?"

Sister Rosa, who had stood listening, clapped her hands. "*Yes!* He is tall as his guardian is. I believe he could pass for sixteen."

After Stanley left, Mother Clare and Sister Rosa clasped each other's hands joyfully. "I'll talk to her about doing some sewing when it's needed by the store's customers, too. But not as an employee of the store. Go now, Sister, and send them to me."

It would be hard to decide who looked the most pleased with the job interview, Mother Superior, Sister Rosa, Carlotta, or Juan. Happiness radiated in the little office and spilled out into the hallway as the visitors left.

Carlotta rejoiced that she and Juan would have a place to stay, and she would have a job where she was needed. Juan could not believe he might get to work too, and have money of his own. He asked the Mother Superior twice to be sure Mr. Jordan wanted to speak with him as well as Carlotta.

On the way out, Carlotta had to take his arm to slow him down and said, "Let us stop in the store first. It is on our way. I need to speak with the Indian woman."

"Oh, Carlotta —" Juan frowned, looking toward the clinic.

"It won't take long, then we will go to the clinic and talk to Señor Jordan, then we will come back to see Sister Rosa."

"All right. I will wait here at the door for you." He jangled the bell in case the Indian woman had not heard them come in.

Carlotta shot him a half-angry, half-amused glance and started toward the back of the store. She met the Indian woman about halfway and started telling her about going to work at the clinic.

"And I would like to help the store's customers with any sewing they need to have done."

The Indian woman listened stoically without comment to all Eleana said. Then when she had finished and stood looking hopeful, she said only, "My name is Dakota."

"Dakota?"

"My tribe is from Dakota." She nodded her head toward the counter that held the cash register and turned. Carlotta followed her, wondering what she wanted to show her.

Dakota bent and took a wide cardboard box from a shelf somewhere below and set it on the counter. In it were two skirts and one blouse. Each had a note pinned to it. The two skirts needed hemming and had the amount to be shortened and a price. The blouse needed the sleeves cut off and had a mark where the customer wanted them hemmed. It too had a price on it. Carlotta looked at them in wonder.

"Oh, thank you. But, how did you know I would be —"

"I guessed." Dakota's eyes smiled.

"And you have the prices on them, too. I didn't know what to charge."

"Is what other woman charged that was here before," Dakota explained.

Pleased, Carlotta thanked her again and set the box down. "I'll leave these here while we go to the clinic, then I will come back and get them."

Dakota nodded.

When they came back for the box, Carlotta and Juan both had jobs to report to the following morning, and the number of garments in the box had grown to five. Carlotta took the garments, looking gratefully from Dakota to the instructions and prices pinned to them, and handed the empty box back to her to magically grow some more business for her.

Sister Rosa was waiting for them, to show her and Juan where they would sleep. They followed her to another convent building where there were extra rooms for guests.

"The room is not very large, but there is a bed for each of you and some comfortable chairs and a chest for your things next to the closet there. Oh, and you can use the break room to fix your meals and keep a sack of groceries in the refrigerator, if you want to. As you see, there is a half bath here, and there are two full bathrooms on this floor."

"It is very nice." Carlotta stifled the urge to give Sister Rosa a big hug, pumping her hand excitedly instead. Juan was not so inhibited and kissed her on the cheek.

Pleased and happy for them, Sister Rosa chuckled and pointed to the alarm clock on the chest. "This clock is a loan from Stanley Jordan until you can get one of your own." She pursed disapproving lips beneath the merriment in her eyes. "Selfish reasons, I'm afraid."

Juan laughed happily. "He wants us to be at work on time. No fear, Sister, we will be."

Carlotta nodded, thankful for their good luck, her eyes brimming as they met Sister Rosa's. As Sister Rosa left, Carlotta reached for the sewing jobs from the store.

CHAPTER SEVEN

Oliver hummed "Spanish Eyes" as he showered. He scrubbed shampoo into his scalp, his heart beating faster as he looked forward to his date with Eleana.

I'm kissing that woman tonight. Enough time's been sacrificed to propriety. He laughed out loud about Matt calling him Not Proper Ollie.

Well, he was proper to the bone now. He adjusted the water again to rinse his hair. The rush of cold water hit him and dashed further speculation from his mind.

Oliver had called on Eleana every other night since they had met, and it was not enough. He wanted more. More time. More of her. Her beauty, her company, her love. Yes, her love. The thought sobered him. He contemplated marriage, a lasting commitment. He wanted her to be part of his life.

She's the prettiest thing I've ever seen. Yes, come propriety or nosy landladies or what,

I'm going to hold Eleana in my arms and kiss her tonight.

He pictured Eleana's face smiling up at him. *Then I'll know if the softness in her eyes means she feels the same way about me. When I helped her down from that high curb the other night and she brushed against me it was like an electric shock. It was all I could do to let go of her.*

"Hey!" The shout from Matt drowned out the shower. "Just how clean are you planning on getting?"

"That's between me and my soap dish, you big oaf! I'll be out in a little bit."

Matt helped himself to a glass of lemonade and sat down at the kitchen table to wait. It wasn't long before Oliver came in and joined him, carrying his shirt and shoes. Matt stared at all that clean and the shirt Oliver draped carefully over a chair.

"Don't tell me, let me guess. Date with Eleana?"

"Yes. I'd see her every night if she'd let me. And that old dragon she rents from is such a nosy witch," Oliver went on complaining, "I'd have kissed her goodnight —"

"The nosy old dragon?" Matt was at his aggravating best.

"No, you idiot. Eleana. My beautiful

Eleana. That old dragon is always right there when I bring her home. I never get to tell her goodnight alone."

Matt laughed, enjoying Oliver's frustration. "She's taking care of her tenants. She's a careful old dragon. She's protecting them from the likes of you, you horny devil." He laughed, his big shoulders shaking with mirth.

"I tell you, Matt, a little more of this frustration and the dam's gonna bust. I'm going to find a quiet spot somewhere, somehow, tonight, so I can kiss her." He added thoughtfully, "You can tell a lot from a kiss."

"Yeah, you're right about that. But I can tell you now and end your misery." Matt's face got serious. "The lady likes you, Oliver."

"Do you think so, Matt? I mean, nothing serious has ever been said between us. We are usually with someone else, or in a crowd. And I've always been respectful. I know in her country they're not as — as —"

"Fast," Matt supplied. He shrugged. "Maybe they're right. Take it easy. You haven't known each other very long." Something that felt like a furry caterpillar of worry still crawled around Matt's mind. The yet-unanswered questions about what had happened to Eleana's brother told him there was danger there. Carlos Castillo was not the sort to just drop out of sight with no explanation. Something there was not quite right and needed to be explained before Oliver ran headlong into some kind of danger. *Or is it heart-long?* he asked himself, watching Oliver put on his shirt. "Just take it easy and let her get to know you." He grinned. "And all your good points."

"I know that. I'm willing to get to know each other better and, of course, talk over things important to both of us. Or any other thing a couple planning on marriage would talk about." He paused to look at Matt. "But I think I've found the woman I want, if she'll have me."

That sounded scary to Matt, but he hid it with a shrug.

"Oh, it won't hurt you to take your time. And I don't think you've got anything to worry about. You're both the picture of puppy love, a classic example." He made quotation marks with his fingers and grinned at his buddy hobbling around on one leg to get his pants on.

"Well, we'll see."

"Listen, what I came over here to tell you about . . ." Matt leaned back in his chair. "I asked Luke like I said I would about the whereabouts of Carlos Castillo, and all my brother could find out for sure is that he's here legally. So that's one thing we don't have to worry about."

"I wasn't worried."

"Yeah, I know —"

"Eleana said he had his papers and all that, that Carlos has worked here before."

"Uh-huh. Also someone had made a note on the file, Luke said, that he was working at Farrel's Grove."

"That's where Eleana said she thought he was. So he's there after all? Eleana will be glad to hear that. I'll tell her tonight — in some dark, secluded place —" Oliver looked as much like some predatory beast as he could manage with half his mind already occupied.

"Try and concentrate," Matt insisted. "You don't listen. That's not where he is. I told Luke about Farrel's Grove, is why the note was made. He's not there."

"Oh, I see what you mean. It's just still in the file?"

Matt nodded. "The place Eleana said she went to ask about him and they said he and his buddy were gone. No one bothered to change the record — probably didn't know anything else to add."

"And nothing else in the file? Nothing at all has been added or updated?"

"No. You remember she said this Lehandro told her that her brother and his cousin got their things they had left there when they thought they were going to work for him, and then they both left. They didn't tell anyone where they were going. So all I know for sure is he does have the proper papers, but not where he is. Just that much made me feel better. When you told me about her and her brother, it's the first thing I wondered about. So at least he's got his papers."

Oliver's brows with the golden glints in them came together in a worried squint. "Then why did he just disappear? Can't Brother Luke make any educated guesses?"

"No. They don't operate on guesses. He says there are always people coming in to recruit help. All different kinds of help. Some short term, some that need help every year. He and his friend may have gone with one of them."

"What is it you're not telling me?" Oliver turned slowly, narrowing his eyes. "I know you too well. There's something else. Tell me, what is it?"

Matt's answer came out reluctantly. "Some of these recruiters are pretty dirty

115

birds. They talk the men into going with them, then they don't pay them what they promised, or conditions are so bad there should be a better word than just 'bad' to describe them." Matt's eyes met Oliver's as he laid the truth on him. "Inhuman would be closer. Some of these employers don't care if their workers get sick or die. It's nothing to them. There are more workers wading across the river every day and night to take their places."

"Nice folks. I hope he didn't get mixed up in something like that. Is there anything we can do? Or does Luke have any suspects? You got any ideas?"

"No, but Luke has his hands full right now. He will help us. It just may take a while. Right now Luke's got his hands full of inquiries and complaints he has to look into. Someone reported an *hombre* up north of here is recruiting then refusing to pay the men, but it was . . ." Matt frowned, shaking his head, "An anonymous tip."

Oliver frowned. "Anonymous?"

"Yes. Actually he got two or three, the last two hearsay only, but it got his attention that he'd got three of them, even if it was secondhand information, before the list of ones who did give their family names got so long. But all the men do is complain. They

116

won't give names and places and the facts he needs. It's one of those 'there's smoke so there's bound to be some fire' things, and they're working on it. They're trying to trap whoever it is and put an end to the business. But it's darned hard to do. About the only concrete information I have to report is Luke told me he will ask around. You know, people he knows, and see if he can find out who was recruiting around here when Carlos left his other job."

"At least I can tell her you've talked to Luke and he is helping us, that he's working on it. Also, he knows Carlos has his papers. That he's asking around to see who was recruiting when they dropped out of sight is a good start." Oliver nodded his head. "It's the logical thing to do. And there may be more come in about the situation, from those men you said were complaining. Who was that man she said she talked to about Carlos?"

"Lehandro. Mr. Lehandro. I asked Luke about him while I was at it. He told me Lehandro's all right. He's been around a while and has a good reputation. All his business and hiring is always on the up and up. He's legit. Carlos and his friend should have stayed with him. But I know what you're thinking, and Lehandro probably either

117

won't know, or might just not tell us, who was around recruiting unless he knows for sure there is something bad going on."

"And I guess from what you said, it would just be more hearsay even if he would. But at least there's hope." Oliver tried to find something encouraging to tell Eleana. "At least Luke is helping us and has found out a few things. Since he's going to ask around to see who was recruiting here, he's bound to turn up something, don't you think?"

Matt nodded as he got up and turned with his hand on the door. He grinned. "Give my regards — or something — to the old dragon."

Eleana had showered to cool off and was almost finished dressing when there was a knock on her door. She opened it a crack and saw her landlady standing there.

"Yes?"

"I have a message for you, Eleana. May I come in?"

The sixtyish face was close to the door as if trying to see in. Eleana paused, feeling somehow that her privacy was being invaded.

"A message?" Eleana buttoned the last two buttons of her blouse as she spoke.

"Yes. It came just before you got home

from work. I brought it up to you as soon as I could. May I come in?"

Reluctantly, Eleana opened the door and the "old dragon" came in, looking at everything from the neatly made bed to the articles on Eleana's dressing table.

Eleana didn't invite her to sit down, resenting her curiosity. "What is the message?"

"This came for you by a messenger I had never seen before." The old woman's tone of voice implied that was a bad thing. She pulled an envelope from her apron pocket. "It is sealed," she added, looking at it again as she handed it to Eleana.

Eleana saw it was not an envelope but a doubled sheet of paper. The message was folded three times and sealed with candle wax at both ends and in the middle. *So nosy people like you could not peek in,* Eleana thought as she took it and inspected the three seals as closely as her landlady must have. The woman waited expectantly.

Holding the message in one hand, Eleana opened the door with the other as she forced a smile to her lips. "Thank you," she said sweetly, and stood waiting for her visitor to leave.

Disappointed but knowing she was beaten, the old dragon slowly walked out the door and it was closed firmly behind her.

Sitting down at her dressing table, Eleana carefully broke the seals and unfolded the paper. The first thing she noticed was that it was written in Spanish. Her hand tightened on the sheet as she read.

It's from Carlotta!

She read and reread the message. There seemed to be so much that Carlotta only hinted at.

But she is all right, and I know where she is. Eleana said a brief prayer of thanks and crossed herself before picking up her purse. She put the note in it, knowing her nosy visitor would be back to read it if she left it lying around.

She looked out her narrow window of her room, puzzling over all the questions in her mind and wondering what she should do. Oliver would be there soon.

I must go to Carlotta and make sure she is all right and find out how she came here. That is the first thing I must do. She tried to put thoughts of any further action out of her mind until later. She considered Oliver, fearing what he would think if Carlotta was really here and in hiding, as all those seals told her she must be.

Eleana carefully locked her door and tested it, not that it would do much good when the old dragon had a key. She smiled to herself at the name Oliver had given her.

The landlady was sitting on the porch, watching everyone who came in, went out, or passed by along the street. Eleana felt an unexpected wave of pity for her. The old dragon hadn't much else to interest her. She looked up as Eleana came to her.

"This message," Eleana started, and hesitated a second, not knowing what to say, wanting to tell her only what was necessary.

"I must leave, but Mr. Avery is coming to see me tonight. Would you please tell him that I have been called away? Tell him that I am very sorry and that I hope to see him tomorrow or some other time. Would you mind to give him that message for me?"

"No, I don't mind at all. I will be glad to." Her eyes studied Eleana, "If I can be of any help —"

"No." Eleana answered quickly, ashamed of her unspoken opinion of her landlady, in the face of an offer to help her. "But thank you. Just, please, give Mr. Avery my message." She turned and hurried down the steps, not looking back.

Approaching the rooming house porch to call for Eleana, Oliver saw the old dragon waiting. She had been sitting in her usual chair on the porch but got up when she saw him coming from across the street. She met him at the top of the steps, looking smug, and delivered the message she had for him.

"*Not here?* What do you mean, she's not here?" Oliver realized he was putting too much pressure on the old dragon's arm and abruptly released it, looking apologetic.

The old dragon rubbed her arm and peered defiantly up at him. *Young smart aleck,* she thought.

"All I know is she got a message. A very mysterious message it was. It was *sealed,*" she taunted him. "With candle wax. In *three* places! I took it up to her, then came back down here. Then in a little while, she came down and told me she had been called away." She tilted her head, hoping to learn something about this mysterious message. "She said to tell you she was sorry."

Sorry? The word struck Oliver like a bullet. It sounded so final, his mind panicked. Oliver stood silent a few seconds, wondering what could have called Eleana away. Then, realizing how much the spiteful woman was enjoying his misery, he shrugged.

"Thank you. I'll — I'll see her another time." He turned quickly and went back down the steps.

She didn't have to be so darned glad about it. And a message sealed with candle wax in three places? Sounds like something out of a comic book, or maybe an old suspense novel like my mom used to read. She must have made that part up, the old — the old — oh, hell, who cares about her?

The landlady would have enjoyed the misery his suspicions put him through.

What kind of message could have made her leave like that, sealed or not? Something sudden. She said she had been "called away." And she left right away, too. What could have called her away so suddenly, what or who?

Oliver's tortured mind began to picture handsome Latin men. Everyone he'd seen in Las Flores and at the movies crowded into his mind. Each one of them a movie star with a sword in his hand, looking like Zorro. Oliver's hands clenched in his pockets, and his heart felt like it was held in a punishing vise.

Sealed, she said. Maybe it was. She was so positive, and so tickled about it, the old bat. A romantic message sealed with candle wax — sealed in three places. Something the one who sent it didn't want anyone else to see. Sounds like something right out of one of Joanna's romance paperbacks. But it can't be. No! No, she would have told me if there was someone else — wouldn't she? She and I, we've not had much time to talk to each other, to be alone.

No inquisitor or torturer could have done the exquisitely painful job on Oliver that he was doing on himself.

Eleana! Who could have sent that message to her? Or do I have any right to ask? Just because she let me hold her hand and looked at me with those big brown eyes, I thought we were attracted to each other. That it was mutual, all these feelings I have. But we never talked about the other people in our lives. Only her brother, the one that brought us together, that gave me an excuse to see her.

His mind was so full of questions and misery, he didn't pay much attention to where he was going. He just wound up at Matt's house from force of habit. His car parked and his mind registered that it knew where to go, like an old horse. He fought down a hysterical laugh at himself and his situation. Oliver's thoughts had worked their way from disappointment, anger, and hurt, to worry. All kinds of far-out possibilities presented themselves to his imagination.

Maybe some low-life thug threatened her. A pretty girl, more or less alone here — I'll kill him! Whatever that message was, it was either important or scary. She left as soon as she got it. He banged on Matt's screen door, sounding as desperate as he felt.

Joanna answered the door, started to speak, then stopped. She tore her gaze from the sight of Oliver's tormented face and left for the back porch as Matt came past her.

"Looks like you two might want to talk." She bobbed her head at Oliver and hurried out the back door.

Matt stopped a couple of feet from Oliver, his mouth open, eyes squinting at him. Something was wrong. Bad wrong. Oliver just stood there.

"Earthquake alert? Old dragon bite you?" Matt's questions poured out in search of the problem he needed to help Oliver fix. Or was it that he needed to fix Oliver? He got no answers, but he kept trying.

"Been diagnosed with terminal crud? You've lost your *mind?*"

Oliver's face crumpled. He looked like a sunflower or some other towering plant that had been out in the heat without water too long and was going to wilt, right there, right then. Matt quickly reached out to put his arm around him and led him to a chair.

"Here, sit down and tell Father Matthew all about it."

Eleana tried not to look worried as she left, feeling the landlady's curious eyes on her back.

I hope she didn't think it was strange that I left in such a hurry. I had to get away before she started asking questions. She really is a very nosy person, Oliver is right about her.

She smiled at the thought of her Golden One. *I will have to tell him something of why I had to leave, but I cannot tell him about Carlotta. I have to go and see for myself that she is all right. Then when I see him, I will tell him . . . oh, I don't know what I can tell him. I cannot betray them, Carlotta and her baby. But oh, to do such a thing now. Ah, no matter. They are here. I must go make sure she is all right.*

As she approached the bus stop, she saw the bus coming and ran to catch it. Another woman, along with a few others and some children were waiting for the bus as it pulled over.

She joined them as they started boarding the bus and stood with one foot on the step.

"Please," Eleana asked hopefully. "Does this bus go out to Santa Maria de Las Flores?"

"Yes, it does. It and the clinic are the last stops on this route."

"Oh, that is good. Thank you. I have some tokens here." Eleana got on the bus and fished in her oversized shoulder bag. Her office manager had suggested she get the bus tokens, though she hadn't had occasion to use them until now and didn't know how many it would take.

She held several tokens in her hand, glancing at the driver.

"Just put one in that slot there, miss," the driver said, smiling patiently. He waited for her to get settled in the first seat before pulling the big bus from the curb, and her heart's frightened fluttering calmed a little.

Eleana looked briefly at the scenery passing by, but her mind and heart were too full of questions to notice much. It seemed like a long drive to her. The note had let her know where Carlotta was, but it had raised even more questions than it answered.

All Carlotta told me was that she is at the convent. How did she get there? There is only one way she could get there that I know of. But how could Juan let her do such a dangerous thing? She was probably afraid to say too much in the note. Just calling the convent "Our Lady." And what is this sewing she was hinting about? Well, no matter. I will know in a little while. I wonder if she might know where Carlos is. But no, how could she? I will just have to wait until I see her.

"Miss?" The bus driver's voice interrupted her thoughts.

"Yes? Are we almost there?"

"Yes, it's just a few more blocks. I wanted to tell you, the last bus will be at the convent at nine o'clock. There will be no more busses after the one at nine o'clock."

"Oh, thank you. I did not know that. And I will need to ride back."

The driver stopped in front of the clinic and opened the door. Eleana smiled. "Thank you," she said again.

The bus pulled away and Eleana gazed at the convent, wondering where to look for Carlotta. A boy crossing the concrete from the store to the clinic caught her attention. With a start, she recognized him.

"Juan!"

The boy stopped dead still, then turned to face her.

"Eleana!" Juan cried her name joyfully and ran to meet her.

They embraced happily. Eleana kissed his forehead and ruffled his dark hair.

"I got Carlotta's note. But there is a lot it did not tell me." Her eyes accused Juan.

Juan was unhappy, feeling guilty under his

big sister's questioning eyes. He bowed his head before answering.

"I know. And I know what you are going to say. But . . ." He looked up at her, trying to make her understand. "What else could I do, Eleana? She was going to come here. She wants so much for the baby to be born here." Juan looked away, across the walk to the clinic where Carlotta was still working.

"I do know it was dangerous to come as we did. I have heard of the people who died or were robbed or were never heard of again, so their people do not know what happened to them. I was frightened, for her and the *niño* and for me, too." He looked up at Eleana, a tear threatening to spill over. "But I promised Carlos I would take care of her. I could not let her come alone."

His misery was written all over his face and drooping shoulders, and Eleana relented. Her heart warmed to her little brother.

"I know Carlotta can be very determined. She is a strong-minded girl. But Carlos thought he was leaving her safe, with Raquel's house so close and you there with her, to call Raquel and Paco if you needed help."

"Ah, Carlos. Do you think he will beat me badly?" Juan's face mirrored the fear of

129

punishment and guilt in him at the thought of facing Carlos.

"Yes. I think he will beat you badly." Eleana laughed and rumpled his hair, her love showing. "You took an awful chance, coming the way you did. Just thank the good Lord you are both safe."

"We thank Him every night, Eleana," Juan told her solemnly.

"Where is Carlotta? I must see her and talk to her."

"She is working in the clinic. And I am working too," he added proudly.

"But, you are only fourteen years old!" Her eyes demanded the truth. "You did not tell them this, did you?"

"No, I did not tell them. When he — the man at the clinic — talked to us, he talked mostly to Carlotta and I pretended I did not understand too much." He looked away briefly, ashamed of the near-lies involved. "And they are in such need for help. And I am doing the work well, Eleana. I am a very good worker for them."

"I am sure you are." Eleana nodded, proud of him, her heart aching for her little brother, who had suddenly had such grown-up problems thrust upon him. "It's just that all of us love you and we worry about you. This was a *very* dangerous thing

130

to do, Juan. More than you can know, for both of you."

He nodded. "I think Carlotta does not have long to wait now. She said maybe two or three weeks until the baby comes. That is why she sent the note to you. We —" Juan studied the concrete between his feet. "We did not try to contact Carlos."

They do not know we cannot find him. This is one thing they will not be worried about, and Oliver and his friends will surely find Carlos soon.

Juan looked up, his expression brighter. "Carlotta and the baby, they are safe and well cared for here, Eleana."

Eleana sighed. "Yes, I am sure she is. I am glad she is here at the clinic. Where is she? Do you think I can talk to her now?"

"Yes. Come, I will take you there. She is folding linens and she can talk." He started toward the clinic and Eleana had to hurry to keep up with him.

Juan led the way to a side door at the clinic and they went down a hallway toward the back of the building. Then he disappeared into a doorway, and Carlotta stepped out to greet Eleana.

She came with open arms to embrace her, and Eleana kissed her on both cheeks, a few tears spilling over as she looked at her.

"I hoped you got my note. I asked at your office, told them I am your sister-in-law, so I got your address. I was afraid about sending it, but I had to let you know I am here." She brushed the already-drying tears away as she spoke. "We are here." She smiled through misty eyes, caressing her unborn child.

"I was glad to know where you are and that you are all right. We were so worried about you. I can tell Raquel now that you are well, and it is good you are here at the clinic. She was so frightened to find you and Juan gone. I must tell her as soon as I can."

"Yes, tell her I am all right. But do not tell where I am or anything more. The phone is at *la tienda* —"

"Yes, yes, I know. Raquel will understand." Eleana dismissed her worries. "Juan tells me he is working too?"

"Yes, both of us are working here and saving our money. And Eleana, the *sewing!* I have so much to tell you." She looked at the clock above the door. "As soon as I finish folding the linen we can leave, and we will go over to the convent and talk."

"Let me help you. Where did Juan disappear to?"

Carlotta looked at the piece of linen she was folding. "Here, fold them like this." She glanced at the door. "Juan went back to work, but he will come and join us. We do not have to wait for him."

Talking as they worked, with no one to overhear, Carlotta related the adventures they had had getting there. About hiding in the little grotto below the water line and the map that Carlos had made and the small, hidden cave.

"Oh, Carlotta, you might have been caught! The patrol might even have shot at you! And the long walk, and you are lucky there was no one at the place where the cave was. People have been found *dead* in such places. *Robbed and left to die.* Carlotta, you must promise me you will *never* do such a dangerous thing again. Even now you could be caught, then you might not be able to get the proper papers, after doing a thing like this." Eleana cast a fearful look at the door.

"I know, Eleana. And I won't. I won't have to do this again. My baby will be born here, as I prayed he would."

Eleana bit her lip, not looking at Carlotta. *I cannot tell her we do not know where Carlos is. She has enough to worry about already. Oh, I pray Oliver's friend can find him for us soon. I pray Carlos is safe and well, and Jorge, too . . .*

She kept her eyes down on the folding work so Carlotta could not read the worry in her eyes, the unanswered questions that still haunted her.

"I know you think I should not have taken the chance in coming here. But, Eleana, I tried to do this by the rules they told us about. I went to apply for my papers as soon as Carlos left, when he had been gone about two days and I was caught up with the things I had to do at home. There was so much paperwork and questions to answer, as well you know." She looked up at Eleana.

"Yes, I know. It was the same for me. I had all the same questions and the paperwork to fill out, too, and the waiting." Eleana nodded, feeling sympathetic.

"Well, I answered all the questions and requirements the best I could. Then, when all of it was finished, they told me it would take even more time for me to get my papers. I could not wait, I had to come while I was able to come, Eleana."

Carlotta caressed her unborn child again. "Carlos is trying to keep a good work record and to get to come here legally, but for my baby, I want him —"

"Or her," Eleana gently reminded her.

"Or her." Carlotta smiled. "I want so much for my baby to be born here so he or she can say this is the place of his birth. It will be on the birth certificate he will have all his life. Do you understand?"

"Yes, Carlotta. But I still think it is a very frightening thing you did. I'm just glad you and Juan are both all right." She patted Carlotta's hand. "I am to call Raquel at the store tomorrow and I will tell her you are well and safe. That is all she wants to know."

"Maybe they have had some word from Carlos by now, since he is in Las Flores. Though he never has much time to write when he is away working. I contacted only you." Guilt lowered Carlotta's eyes as she spoke. "I do not mean to tell him I am here until the baby is born."

Eleana didn't answer, her eyes on the linens she was folding.

Carlotta clasped her hands. "When he sees our baby safe and born here, he will be too happy to be upset with me for coming here."

Eleana did not smile. "I don't know about that, Carlotta. It is frightening to me only to *think* about it. It was a very dangerous thing to do. For you and the baby, and Juan, too."

"But we are safe and here, and the baby will be born soon, and Carlos will be with us soon. Maybe he has written by now, or you have been in touch with him? That is one reason I did not write to you until now. But no matter, we will be together again soon."

Again, Eleana didn't answer, her heart heavy. She hoped Carlotta was right.

Carlotta put the linens in a linen closet close by and, chattering happily, did not notice how quietly and slowly Eleana followed her out as they left.

"Oh, and Eleana, tell Raquel too, if the permit papers do come for me, or other papers, to keep them for me. I doubt they will come, but tell her to keep them if they do come."

"I will, Carlotta." Eleana could assure her of that with honesty. "I will tell her tomorrow."

Juan was waiting for them in the patio, watching the goldfish in the pond. As soon as they came out the clinic door he hurried to them.

"Carlotta! Eleana!" His broad smile reflected Eleana's.

Carlotta touched Juan's unruly hair affectionately. "We use the break room to fix our meals, Eleana. Tonight we are having Juan's favorite, hot dogs and beans!"

Juan ran ahead of them and had two cans of beans out waiting for them.

Carlotta laughed, holding up the beans.

"I'm glad they are easy to fix." She flipped a dishcloth at Juan.

Eleana laughed with them as Juan showed how familiar he was with the microwave and put the wieners in.

"It seems you have everything you need here, Carlotta. You and Juan, as they say here, you have it made." Eleana smiled. "I am impressed."

They talked happily as they ate, and Eleana was amazed at how many wieners Juan could eat and manage to talk at the same time.

"I have been to the park where Carlotta and I stopped on the way here, Eleana. They have a place roped off to swim and they have a place to play baseball, too." His eyes sparkled with excitement. "I stay well back where I won't be noticed, although there are many there who could be my cousins. I don't think I would be noticed."

He paused to take another bite. "But the games are fun to watch. I like to go there when I am not working."

Carlotta and Eleana's eyes met. They knew how much he would like to play. Silently, both hoped someday Juan would not have to worry about being noticed and could join in the games.

"Are these only children who come together to play, or is it teams that come from somewhere near here?" Eleana asked, making polite conversation.

"Right now, I think anyone can play. Yes," Juan said thoughtfully. "I think that anyone can come and maybe be asked to play. But there is a man there who organizes them into teams and they play against each other." He looked at Eleana, and she could tell he was impressed with the man. "They call him Matt, and I heard someone say he is a coach at the school in Las Flores." Juan beamed. "He must know *everything* about baseball!"

Eleana had paled as she listened, and Carlotta touched her hand. "What is it, Eleana? Are you all right?"

"Yes, yes. I am all right. But, Juan, this man they call Matt, is he about as tall as Carlos, and does he have blond or dark blond hair?"

"Yes, and his hair is very curly, and it is short. I bet he never has to comb it," Juan answered, puzzled as well as envious.

Eleana did not explain. Instead, she asked Carlotta, "Are you about ready for us to clear away our dishes and go where we can talk?"

"Yes, it won't take us very long." Carlotta hurriedly picked up their plates, and with

Eleana and Juan helping, they were through in no time. Juan cast two or three questioning looks at Eleana to no avail.

Carlotta led them to the room she and Juan shared, hurrying and not speaking either.

Going in, Eleana praised the room and Carlotta's housekeeping, then Carlotta closed the door firmly and asked her, "What is it? Why did you look so frightened when Juan told you about the games in the park?"

CHAPTER EIGHT

Eleana knew she must weigh her answers very carefully, but she must also warn them not to let Matt know who they were. She and Carlotta pulled their chairs close together, and Juan sat on his bed near them, listening.

"Carlotta," Eleana began, "the man named Matt, I know him."

Juan brightened; he liked Matt. But the expression was short-lived, because Eleana looked so grim.

"His name is Matt Jacobs and his brother, he is the sheriff here in Las Flores. And he also sometimes works with the INS, the Immigration and Naturalization Service."

She looked at Juan, her expression serious. "It is good you stayed back and watched the games. Matt is the coach at the school, yes, and he is a good man. But you can't be too careful, and I know his brother works for all the good of the people here and he is a good man, as Matt is. He tries to help everyone, he told me."

"He told you?"

"Yes. Matt told me." Eleana spoke slowly, picking her words carefully, talking to both of them. "I have met a very nice man here since I have come and have been working here. I have had dinner with them. This is how I know him. Know Matt, and know about his brother, the sheriff."

Carlotta's face lighted up at the mention of Eleana having dinner with the very nice man.

"Ah! A nice young man. Tell us about him, Eleana. And do not be afraid for Juan. He knows how to stay out of trouble." Carlotta pressed for more information about Eleana's nice young man.

"We met at the mall, and I did not go out with him to have dinner alone. His friends, Matt and Joanna, were there to chaperone us. It was all very proper, Carlotta."

"*Sí,* I am very glad it was, as you say, all very proper, Eleana." Carlotta smiled. "But the look on your face when you talk about him, that gives away your secret thoughts. You very much like this young man, no?"

Eleana didn't hesitate long; her lips insisted on smiling as she thought of Oliver. His eyes, his concern about helping her find her brother, the gold in his hair.

"Yes. Yes, I do. He is . . . oh, I don't know if I can describe him for you. He is about the same height as Matt, maybe just a little taller, and he is a little more slender."

"Slender. Golden hair," Carlotta repeated. Eleana blushed at Carlotta's knowing look, but continued. "And his hair is about the same color, like honey, except it has streaks in it the sun has made, and it gleams like gold, Carlotta. When I think about him, I call him my Golden One." She smiled, her happiness radiating from her. It was good to have someone she could talk to about Oliver.

"And he likes you? He has come to see you many times?"

"We are both working, but we do see each other very often. He teaches art at the college here."

"Oh, an artist," Juan observed. "That is bad. They starve in attics and no one knows their names until they are dead a hundred years."

Eleana and Carlotta turned dark looks on him and he hastily added, "But he teaches art. That is good. Teaching is honorable work, and has a steady paycheck." Juan looked hopefully at them to see if this had redeemed him.

Eleana forgave him and Carlotta explained, tilting her head toward Juan. "Since the man at the clinic has let him work, Juan has his mind on money most of the time."

"I never had a chance to make any money at home," Juan protested. "I like it!"

"That reminds me, this talk of money." Carlotta pointed to the chest of drawers. "I have made a lot of money sewing for people."

"This is what I did not understand when I read your note, about using your needle?"

"I could not write too much. I was afraid. But I am doing some sewing, Eleana. For customers who buy things at the store, and students at the college too. And now that they know there is someone who can sew at the store, some of the women from the town bring me things too. When they pay me I stick the money I get in one of our sacks in the chest over there. I do not know very much yet about the money. I will try to count it when we start home. I know there is always enough there for me and Juan to get what we need and not have to do without anything we need to buy." She turned to Juan.

"Show her your new shoes, Juan."

Juan stuck out his feet. "They are called athletic shoes. Anyone can run well in these." He said it proudly and turned his feet for his shoes to be admired.

After looking at the box that held Carlotta's sewing, Eleana glanced out the window. "This is good, and I feel better now that I know you are here safely and working. And the sewing is good too, to buy the things you need. I know you need to be doing your sewing for tomorrow, and I had better go anyway. The driver of the bus told me the last bus stops here at nine o'clock, and it is after eight-thirty now. I had better go out and wait, so I will not miss it."

"We will go and wait with you then. I'm glad you got my note, and we are so happy to see you. Thank you for coming to us." They hugged each other before Eleana opened the door to leave.

Outside, they sat on one of the concrete benches in front of the clinic, watching the sunset's last gamut of beautiful colors, and talked until the bus came.

"I will not be coming again unless you need me. We don't want to call attention to your being here and have people asking questions. But you can contact me at the number where I work or the pay phone where I live. And tomorrow I will tell Raquel you are all right and safe."

The bus ride home was much more enjoyable than the ride to the convent had been. Eleana felt as if a burden had been lifted from her shoulders now. She had seen for herself that Carlotta and Juan were safe, and was comforted. She smiled to herself, remembering Juan's new shoes and how proud he was of his job.

So that is two of my family who are safe and well. And after all, Carlos and Jorge are grown men. Surely they are all right too, and we will hear from them soon. I know Raquel will be overjoyed when I speak to her tomorrow. Her hopes rose, too, that Raquel might have had a letter from Carlos by this time.

The bus stop was about two blocks from her rooming house, but it was still light enough to see her way at that hour. She glanced ahead toward the front porch when she got in sight of the house and noted that her landlady had already gone in. The night was quiet, and the streetlight made a little puddle of light on the sidewalk.

Before she could thank the good Lord for that, she heard someone call her name.

"Eleana! Here!"

She stopped, squinting in the murky dusk and saw a car parked across the street. A man stood beside it.

"Oliver!" She crossed the street to him and looked up, wondering why he was there at that hour.

He reached out for her hands and she placed them in his, still not speaking, half afraid of the questions he might ask.

"I just wanted to know you were all right. That you got home all right," he amended.

"Yes, I'm fine, Oliver. Did you get my message that I had to leave?"

"Yes, I got it." Oliver smiled wryly. "I think the old dragon really enjoyed giving it to me, too."

"Oh, I know how she is. Did she tell you I hoped to see you tomorrow night?"

"No. Somehow, she forgot to mention that part. She just said that you got some kind of message that called you away and you had to leave."

"There wasn't time to do anything else, Oliver. I'm sorry I had to leave a message with her."

"I'm bruised but not beaten," Oliver said, grinning. "I don't suppose you're going to tell me where you had to go?" He paused hopefully.

"No." Her eyes begged him to understand. "I can't, Oliver."

"Can't, or won't?" He stiffened, standing straighter.

"Can't. I would like to. But — there are others involved." She looked down at the cracked sidewalk, not wanting to meet his eyes.

"Others." He repeated it, looking like the word tasted bad on his tongue.

Oliver stood there holding her hands, still waiting for some attempt at an explanation. But she said no more, and he was the one who broke the silence.

"Well, do you suppose those 'others' could spare you to me tomorrow night?"

Part of him hoped that didn't sound sarcastic. The rest of him growled inside, *I feel sarcastic.* He waited for her answer.

"Yes, I'm glad to say they can, Oliver."

Her Spanish eyes lit up, maybe because he was there. He hoped it was because he was there. And she had such a bewitching grin. It had become darker as they stood there talking. Impulsively, he pulled her to him and kissed her on the lips.

Surprised when their lips met, Eleana responded and her arms went around him, yielding to the kiss they had both waited for. Oliver wanted her so much it hurt. He held her close and kissed her lightly again before he stepped back.

She was breathless, surprised and a little embarrassed at her own reaction to his embrace.

"I'm glad you're safely home now. I'll see

you tomorrow night."

Eleana nodded, still a little shaken, but happy about the kiss. She moved toward the street.

"I'll stay here and wait till you get inside."

On the porch, Eleana turned as she opened the door, and Oliver waved from beside the car. There was no sign of the old dragon, and Eleana could see him waiting there to see her safely inside. She smiled into the night that had turned out so well for her.

Matt was sitting on the front porch when he saw Oliver's car stop in front of the house. He sat and waited until Oliver sat down beside him.

"Where's Joanna?" Oliver glanced back at the lights inside the house.

"She's trying out a new cookie recipe or something in the kitchen."

"Oh."

"And to what do I owe the pleasure of your company?" Matt inquired. "A late bulletin, maybe?"

Oliver hesitated, not answering.

Matt gave Oliver a shrewd look. "I'd guess from your general attitude, there's some fairly good news in this soap opera?"

"Yes and no." Oliver couldn't stop his

telltale grin.

"Don't be so damned aggravating. What happened? Have you seen Eleana again? And did you kiss her or not?"

"Yes. I've seen her. She left a message that she'd been called away."

"Called away? That needs clearing up. You said you'd seen her?" Matt raised his eyebrows.

"Yeah, it was a jolt to me, too. But she was gone when I got there so there wasn't anything I could do about it. When I got there to pick her up, the landlady — the old dragon — told me Eleana got some sort of message and had to leave."

Matt scooted down on the next step and waited for scene two in the melodrama. He leaned back on his elbows.

"I behaved like a real jerk and parked in sight of her rooming house until she came home." He stopped to glare at Matt. "And if you ever tell anybody, I'll *swear you lied!*"

"Okay, okay, cut the small talk and threats. What happened? And you'd better start at the beginning. I'm easy to confuse."

"Okay. First thing was, I got there and the old dragon told me Eleana got a message and had to leave. The old bat really enjoyed delivering the message, more than I can describe. I think she just likes to see people suffer. Like pouring salt on a snail. You'd have to see the old dragon to understand how she loved giving me that message."

"Enjoyed delivering message," Matt repeated, musing half to himself.

"Not just a plain old message. She told me, as if it tasted good, that this message was *sealed* with candle wax."

"Oh-ho! The plot thickens." Matt hooted, waiting for chapter two. "So what did you do next?"

"I thought the candle wax was a little much, too. Anyway, I went back there, to the rooming house, about the time it got dark, and waited."

"Waited for this competition with the candle wax that can write." Matt got as close to a laugh as he dared to get without having his information cut off.

"There wasn't a thing funny about it. I didn't feel funny. Anyway, I sat there across from the house where she lives and waited. Sat there till just before it got good and dark. And then I saw her coming."

"Her, you say. Not them?"

"Her."

"Walking?"

"Yes, she was walking."

"Walking. Alone. Did she see you?"

"I don't think so. I called to her. She came

across the street and we talked." Oliver looked serious. "We talked, but she didn't tell me anything."

"Women are good at that." Matt nodded philosophically. "Did you ask or did she say where she'd been?"

"I asked her if she was going to tell me, and she wouldn't. Just apologized for leaving a message with the old dragon."

"Are you going to see her tomorrow?"

"Yes." Oliver grinned into space like the village idiot.

Matt studied the imbecilic trance on Improper Ollie's face. "You kissed her, didn't you?"

Oliver wrinkled his brow. "Yes and no."

"That's not an answer. You either did or you didn't."

"I mean, it just happened. I kissed her, but just once. I wanted to grab her like a drowning man on a log, but I didn't."

"Oh, *Gawd!* You're in love!" Matt placed his hand on his heart in mock sympathy.

"Haven't you ever heard of respect? Fat lot of understanding I get from my friends . . ." The rest of his mumbling was too low to understand.

"Well, how about it? Is the chemistry mutual, or could you tell if it's love for her?"

"Yes. That is, I *think* it's love."

"Told you. Remember, I told you." Having finally settled that, Matt changed the subject. "By the way, if she asks, we still haven't heard anything about the whereabouts of Carlos and Jorge." Matt rearranged the way he was draped across the steps. Oliver waited.

"But between us, Luke told me he's had inquiries about quite a few other men. People keep coming in to the station. Their stories are the same as in the case of Carlos and Jorge. The men have their papers in order and were working somewhere or supposed to be, then they left, and their people haven't heard anything from them and are asking about them, trying to find them."

"Hmm, that doesn't sound good, does it?" Oliver looked worried.

"No, it doesn't. There are sleazy characters here to cheat or use them, and then their own countrymen prey on them too. There's no telling where they are or what happened to them. All Luke and his men can do is keep an eye out and listen for what they can pick up. Something's bound to turn up." Matt's face was solemn as he admitted, "But, yeah, it does look bad to me."

"I sure can't tell Eleana that. I'll just say that Luke is still making inquiries."

"He certainly is. Especially now that there

seems to be so many more of them. There must be something dirty going on. Big enough to be noticed, and dirty and under-cover too, or he'd have gotten a line on it by now. Luke's got several names of people who were recruiting about the time Carlos and Jorge left, but there is no way to keep up with all of them. He's checking out the ones he knows about, but it's slow work."

"I'll bet it is," Oliver said thoughtfully as he got up. "Anyway, I just thought I'd let you know what's going on. Eleana's all right anyway, and I'm going to see her tomorrow night."

"And you kissed her," Matt teased.

"Shut up, Matt!"

CHAPTER NINE

As Eleana entered the rooming house, the landlady stuck her head out the kitchen door. Eleana smiled and said good night to her. The old dragon's curious eyes followed her up the stairs, and she was obviously wondering where Eleana had been and with whom.

Eleana felt those eyes on her as she went. Her soft heart felt another twinge of pity as she closed the door without looking back.

She has no one and nothing to occupy her time and attention. I'm glad our family is close and loving, even if I can't find them all. She smiled at herself, trying to find her family, her hopes on Oliver and his friends.

Eleana washed her face and neck with cool water and her crisp cotton nightgown felt good against her skin as she pulled it on. She fell asleep thinking of her handsome Oliver and dreamed of Carlotta smiling about her new baby being born in the

United States. She smiled in her sleep about Juan admiring his new shoes. It comforted her that Carlos would be proud of him. Tired, dreaming fitfully, but knowing Carlotta and Juan were safe, Eleana slept.

Carlos and Jorge worked side by side in the stifling heat making the big wooden shipping crates. Both were tired, dirty, miserable, and more than a little discouraged.

Carlos looked around to make sure no one could hear and took the precaution of speaking to Jorge in English, his voice low.

"Jorge, there are two or three more men missing. I can't place who they are, there are still so many in here. But I've been counting for several weeks. And now I'm sure there are three less men here than there were on this shift two days ago."

"Maybe they are on another shift?" Jorge spoke without conviction, trying to convince himself as well as Carlos. "I think sometimes they change the twelve-hour shifts. But maybe that is why they change them, to make up for the ones who are missing, or so the rest of us won't notice they are missing."

They looked at each other then, not wanting to face the truth, but uneasy. Jorge spoke first, from his heart and from the guilt he felt. "I'm sorry I got you into this . . . this hell hole, Carlos."

Carlos protested quickly. "It is not your fault, Jorge. The money looked good to me as it did to you. I did not have to come." He paused, looking cautiously around them. "But we will not make this mistake again. We will go back and work for Señor Lehandro at Farrel's Grove, or wherever they are working next time."

Jorge drew in a ragged breath and coughed, then took a deep breath. "I do not know if there will be a next time. Look around you, my cousin. Look at the others. Look at *us!*" Jorge nearly broke down, and his lip quivered.

"We must get through this and get back to report the conditions here. What Mr. Mansfield said is not true. He has not paid us but half what he promised, sometimes not even close to half. And we are only allowed water to wash ourselves once a week."

Jorge looked sideways at the men closest to them. "And the food. Whatever it is, it must affect the others as it does us. You see the others? Their clothes hang on them like ours do on us."

"The only good thing about it is they take the mail once a week. The pay is so low now, it's a good thing we put both letters in one."

Jorge's face showed the bitterness he felt. "They don't pay us what they promised, but they never miss a chance to make money for themselves. A dollar for every postcard or letter. And the little bar of soap you bought. It looks like the ones they had in that motel we stayed in that time. And they charged five dollars for it! No wonder we are starved and dirty."

"They, or some of the other workers maybe, are stealing from us, too, Jorge. It is a good thing we sewed the money we got into our clothes. One of the ones who is missing today is the man who was complaining last week about his money being stolen. You remember him? He seemed to be very sick with something, the way he coughed. His name was Enrique."

"Yes, I remember. He is gone, and his friend who was always beside him has been gone a week now."

"There is something else that I worry about, Jorge. My Carlotta. Our baby is due in about two weeks now. I've worked longer than I planned to because the money is so low, but we must leave soon. And I cannot get to Mr. Mansfield to ask him about leaving. I asked to speak with him, but have not been able to yet. And no one has been taken back to Las Flores or anywhere else unless it was at night when we did not know about it."

"We must think of something to do while we are still able to get away from here." Jorge nodded slightly, keeping his eyes on the other men. "And I was hoping . . . do you think there will ever be any money coming from the office in the city? Or was that just a lie he told us? I guess it was a lie." Jorge answered his own question and dropped the board he was holding.

"Yes. He lied to us, Jorge. About the money and the conditions. Everything was a lie." Carlos dropped his voice even lower, leaning a bit closer. "I have a plan, Jorge. It may not do any good, but we are going to have to leave soon anyway. Tell me what you think about it when we get outside and can talk more safely."

Jorge nodded. He was desperate and miserable enough to try anything, and Carlos was his trusted friend as well as his cousin.

Mansfield looked up as Parker opened the screen door. "Going to make your mail run tomorrow, Parker?"

Gene Parker was a corpulent bully who delighted in seeing the men who worked for them suffer. He also liked the mail run because it put money in his pocket and was such a good joke on the ignorant wretches who thought he was actually mailing their foolish letters. It brought a mean smirk to his face just thinking about it.

"Yeah. I hope no more of the ugly dogs wise up to what's going on. It's beginning to cut down on my mail business."

"Don't say that too loud," Mansfield warned. "We don't want any more trouble than we've already got to control." He lowered his voice. "Parker, did you take care of those three problems?"

"Yeah. No problems any more."

"Where?"

"The deepest part of the river past the canyon — where the 'post office' is." He grinned. "When they wash up — if they wash up — it'll be in another state."

"Good. No, ah, evidence of foul play?"

"Naw. Just simple drownings, and no identification on them."

"Good. Always see to that. You sure better see that there's no identification. We don't want them tied to us in any way."

Parker dismissed the matter and changed the subject. "How are we coming on that contract? Do we have much more to do?"

"Not really. A couple of months will finish it. Then we'll apologize nicely to the men and send them packing." Mansfield leaned back, looking satisfied. "We'll take the ones left to within ten miles of Las Flores, being the nice gents that we are." His face fell into a merciless mask that looked as hard as stone. "We'll take them at night. By the time any of them tries to tell anyone where this place is, there won't be anything to find even if they do figure out how to get back."

"There will probably be less than thirty of them left. All the complainers seem to be gone now. But if you think any of them will cause us trouble . . ." Parker looked up and Mansfield hesitated.

He's cold-blooded. He wouldn't mind killing every one of them, Mansfield thought. Aloud he answered, "No, they won't cause us any trouble. The ones that are left, except for a few, are the ones that have no papers, and they're desperate for money. We've got to show that we're paying *some* of them to keep operating. By cutting the number in half, we can show that we paid them what we promised in Las Flores." His smirk was arrogant. "Like I told you, we're nice guys."

"I'm glad you're an expert on all that paperwork and satisfying the government." Parker shook his head. His big feet moved and he leaned his chair back against the wall. "We may have two more for the river though. On the way over here, two of the men, the only ones left with papers besides that young one, stopped me and reminded me they want to talk to you in the morning." Parker gave Mansfield a speculative look. "I don't ever pay any attention till the second request. But it looks like they're going to insist."

"Want to talk to me, do they? Two of them? We can handle that. Who are they?"

"Two good workers, worse luck. Carlos Castillo and Jorge Brazos."

Sheriff Luke Jacobs came into the building and sighed. His shirt was wet with perspiration and the air conditioning felt good.

He went into his office and looked at all the problems that had been laid on his desk while he was gone. He groaned and turned away. He headed for the break room to have a cold drink and brace himself to face them.

"Hi. Got back without melting, I see." One of the secretaries waved from an office door. She looked crisp and neat; he wondered how women managed that.

"Just barely, and not by much." He mustered up a wilted grin. "From the looks of my desk, it will take the rest of the day just to sort out by priority what's lying in wait in there."

"Oh, you can handle it. You're tough." She smiled confidently. "I don't know how far down the pile it is." She glanced into the office behind him as he entered. "But yesterday afternoon one of your deputies came in and asked me to put a note on your desk. He wants to see you tomorrow morning before he goes out, if you have time."

"I don't, but I will anyway. Did he say what time? Or tell you what it was about?"

"No, but his shift usually leaves about seven-thirty I think."

"No rest for the weary," Luke said with a deep sigh.

"Carlos! Carlos?" The whisper was urgent, close to his ear.

Carlos stirred, waking from a sleep of sheer exhaustion at the sound of Jorge's voice. His cousin's breathing was hard and rasping as he tried to wake him.

Carlos raised his head, looking around. No one else had heard. He touched Jorge's arm, trying to calm him.

"Jorge, I hear you. What is it?"

"I . . . I woke and went out to relieve myself and got turned around and went the other way, back beyond the old shed —" Jorge shivered as if the heat had an adverse effect on him and he was freezing.

162

Carlos put his hands on both his forearms, holding him tight. "It is all right, Jorge. I am here, and you are all right. Did you have a dream about demons?" He tried to calm him.

"No, no. Carlos, this is bad. But it is not a dream, it is *not!*"

"Shhh! Keep your voice down."

"I went out . . ." Jorge trembled, then controlled himself, taking a breath. "And I got turned around, and I went out farther than we usually go out there. On the other side of the shed where there is nothing but weeds and the straggly trees, and I stumbled over a tree root —"

"Are you all right? Are you hurt anywhere?" Carlos instantly thought of the empty first aid kit he had seen. They could do nothing but perhaps clean any scratch or wound.

"No, no. I am all right. But by then the moon was out and I could see a little. There was a place, a place where a coyote or a dog had been digging —"

"Oh. A hole. And you fell?"

"I fell, but I am not hurt. But . . . but the hole —"

"It is all right, Jorge. You are back now. Calm yourself. It is all right now."

"No. *No,* Carlos, it is *not* all right." His

voice rose slightly.

"Shhh! Jorge." Carlos looked quickly around, but no one seemed to have heard them. "What is not all right?"

"There was a shoe in the hole. A worn-out shoe. I saw it plainly in the moonlight. I saw the shoe and it had a *foot* in it, Carlos. Carlos, someone is *buried* out there!"

"Buried? You are sure?" Carlos frowned into the near darkness around them. None of the others moved.

"Yes, yes. I saw it. I reached out and touched it. It is a shoe with a foot in it. Carlos." The grip on his arm tightened as his voice shook. "The men who are gone now — *madre de Dios!* They have *killed* them! Or, they just died from the sickness, and they hid them — buried them."

Carlos was wide awake now, sitting with his arms on his knees. "Buried them . . ." He murmured as if he still could not believe it.

"What can we do?"

"For right now, the first thing we must do is not let them know we have found out about this. Or our shoes will soon join those other shoes out there."

Carlos put his arm around Jorge's shoulders, leaning close to talk to him. "We must get away from here."

"We must, yes, but how will we do this? They will not let us go. We have not heard of any of the men leaving to go home. We have only seen there are fewer here to work, and no explanation was given."

"And the first ones to go were the ones who asked questions or complained. We must be very careful, Jorge."

Luke was about halfway down the pile of work when he came to the note he was expecting. The deputy's name was Jack Kelly.

Luke chuckled to himself. *He looks more like a José Gonzales.* He pictured Jack's face. *But he's a good, dependable man. Wish I had more like him. Wonder what he wants.*

He shrugged and continued sorting out the accumulated papers. The last four he came to were inquiries from Hispanic Americans making inquiries into the whereabouts of men who were supposed to be working in Las Flores but had not been heard from for a while. He knew about what each one would say from reading the others. But he read each one carefully, hoping to get some kind of clue to why there were so many missing reports all of a sudden.

He frowned as he finished. *It's a regular epidemic of missing persons.*

Carlotta knelt in the chapel, glad there was a mass before she had to go to work. She felt it was all right to go to work on Sunday if she went to mass first. Jesus had lifted the lost lamb out of a hole on a holy day, she reasoned.

She got up very carefully, her hand supporting herself as she rose to her feet.

She was sure Eleana had told Raquel she was safe and well, though Eleana had not mentioned it the last time they had talked.

My people know I am all right. We are safe. Juan is doing well on his job, and soon, soon, we will let Carlos know that Juan and I are here. Surely he will not be too angry, not with the job I have found and the extra money I have made for us. And we will have our beautiful baby to take home with us. I expected Carlos to contact Raquel and Paco at home before this, but Eleana knows we are here. We cannot tell him yet where we are, but soon. Soon . . .

Carlotta frowned, realizing Eleana had not mentioned Carlos. She thought with an affectionate smile that Eleana was probably sparing her feelings, since she knew Carlos would never have approved of her and

Juan's flight to the convent and the chances they had taken. *But, no matter. We will all be together soon.*

Eleana had been back to visit only once, afraid of calling attention to them with too many visits. But Eleana called her every day or two from the office where she worked.

The only thing that worried Carlotta right at the moment was that she hadn't made Juan a sandwich to take with him to the park. He went regularly to the park to swim and to watch the baseball games. When he was not working, that was where he could be found.

He is only a boy, after all, and shouldn't have to work all the time. Carlotta smiled to herself, remembering the fish he had caught for them in the park. Tío Juan!

Juan walked to the park as he always did and stopped at a place where a big rock stuck out into the water. He took off his shoes and socks and washed his feet, then sat dangling them in the water. It was his regular stop to cool off.

The cooling off and the rest were not the only reasons he had for stopping there. He didn't want to get to the play area too soon, before there were many people there.

I will wait until there are lots of people so no

one will notice me. And today, I have the money for a cold drink when the sun gets hot. It would not be good to take Carlotta's money, but I have money of my own now. It is a good feeling.

He looked around, watching everyone who came by, and saw a mother with her two children playing in the edge of the water. He decided it was good to be young and working and to have money in his pocket. His only real worry had been about Carlotta. But she was at the clinic now, with a doctor nearby. He put his shoes back on and walked slowly to the marked-off field where the games were played.

As he got nearer he saw quite a few people seated on the wood and steel bleachers that had been set up for people to watch the games.

I wish I could go and sit there, but, I'd better not.

He walked on past the drink stand and away from most of the people who were watching the boys warming up for the game. There was a shade tree about two-thirds of the way down the field. He sat down and leaned back against the rough bark to watch the activity in the distance. There wouldn't be anyone around to ask questions down here where he sat.

He saw Matt arrive and envied all the fun and fooling around that seemed to be going on as the boys gathered around him, ready to play. Squinting at the group of players and would-be players swarming around Matt, Juan wished he could hear what they were saying, to be part of it, even, perhaps, to play.

Matt scanned the crowd of boys, seeing who was there to play. His keen eyes looked them over. Some of the boys had played before, some were not known to him, and Matt was lining up two teams to get the playing started. He would have liked to have a couple more taller, stronger boys. He looked around again, then spotted Juan sitting under the tree. He summoned one of the boys who had played before and sent him to ask Juan if he wanted to play.

Juan saw the boy coming toward him at a lope and stood up.

Should I run away? No, no. They would wonder about that. Maybe he is not coming to me. Juan looked around, but there was no one behind him or nearby.

The boy stopped beside Juan and told him, "Matt sent me to ask you if you want to play."

Juan was dumbfounded. What would Carlotta say? He stood there undecided and

the boy looked at him, waiting for him to
come back with him.

Juan grinned, his mind made up. "Yes, I
want to play. Thank you."

The boy rolled his eyes at the "thank you"
and gave him a lopsided grin. "Don't mention it. It was Matt's idea."

For a minute as he watched, Matt had
thought the boy might not want to play, that
there was some problem. But then the boy
appeared pleased, as if he were glad he'd
been asked to play. When Juan and the other
boy got near enough, the other boy went to
stand a little distance away, and Matt asked
Juan, "Ever played on a team before?"

Relieved that Matt hadn't asked his name,
Juan answered honestly. "No." He quickly
added, "But I have watched."

"Watched, huh?" Matt grinned. "Well,
you'll catch on quick. It's not very compli-
cated." Matt clapped Juan's shoulder and
sent him to the other team to pitch a few
balls while he looked for more recruits.

When the games started, Juan played well
and Matt noticed he could pitch and that
he could hit just as well as he pitched.

I'll keep an eye on that one.

They played off and on all day, some of
the boys leaving from time to time or to
break for lunch with their families. Matt

tried several times to start a conversation with the new boy, but he was evasive, and good at it. Matt didn't learn anything at all about the boy, not even his name.

Toward the end of the day when they were getting lined out for what would be the last game of the day, Matt looked around for Juan. He was nowhere to be found.

"You see the new kid?" he asked around. No one had noticed when Juan left.

"Drat! He just disappeared. He's awfully shy for some reason. Good hitter though."

At home, Matt told Joanna about finding a good player and chattered about possible recruits until Joanna was ready to go to join Oliver and Eleana.

"I'm sure your new recruit is an absolute *jewel,* but don't you ever get tired of baseball?"

Matt gave it a whole second's serious thought. "Nope!"

Juan had known before the last ball game that Carlotta would get off work by the time he got back, and he timed it just right. When Carlotta came out the clinic door, Juan came from the patio to walk with her.

"Did you enjoy your day off, Juan?"

"Yes. I didn't swim today, Carlotta. I played baseball." His eyes danced.

Carlotta stopped. "You did? But how? Did you tell them who you are and where you live?"

"No, Carlotta. I am not so silly as *that!* I was out in the field, under a tree, and they were looking for people to play and they asked me if I wanted to play. I knew it would look bad to run away, so I played." He looked pleased with himself. "And no one asked me anything, so I didn't *tell* them anything!" He laughed, full of happiness at being able to play and his own cleverness.

"Oh, I see. That was lucky, and I know you wanted to play. But Juan," Carlotta warned seriously, "you know we must be very careful."

"I know," he held the break room door for her. "Next time I go, I will just swim a while and come home. Then maybe I will play the next time, if they ask me. I will not stay around enough for them to start asking me questions."

"They did not ask you anything?" Carlotta found it hard to believe.

"No, nothing. They only asked if I wanted to play. It was such fun, Carlotta, and this man they call Matt, he is a good man, as Eleana says. I like him."

CHAPTER TEN

Matt, Joanna, Oliver, and Eleana went to a movie and stopped at a fast-food restaurant in the mall afterward. They enjoyed being together, and Eleana seemed to feel comforted with friends around her.

Eleana's crisp, white blouse showed off her pretty olive complexion. Joanna thought affectionately as she watched them that Eleana was totally unaware of the effect she had on Oliver most of the time.

As they sat waiting to be served, Oliver smiled at Eleana, holding her hand under the table as they talked.

Oliver could count on a brief goodnight kiss now and felt more confident all the time that Eleana enjoyed the touch of his hand as much as he did hers. But there were those strange disappearances he worried about. It was like a fence or a closed door between them. There was some part of Eleana's life where he was blocked out. He felt she was as glad of his company as he was hers when they were together, but when they were apart, his curiosity worked on what could cause this strange mystery. What could this lack of communication between them mean? That first mysterious message had shaken his hopes, somehow seemed to diminish his importance to her. He couldn't get rid of the discomfort of thinking he didn't matter to her as much as she mattered to him. The mystery of her life worried him. It was like a grain of sand in a pearl oyster.

Matt watched his friend without appearing to, knowing how taken Oliver was with this beautiful woman with the Spanish eyes. There had been two of the mysterious messages now, and Matt was too close a friend not to know there was still something wrong between Oliver and Eleana.

In answer to Matt's questions Oliver simply said he and Eleana were drifting in a happy limbo, probably toward matrimony. Matt now sat watching them as he sipped his drink.

They look happy together to me, Matt decided. *I wish she'd tell him about that mysterious message she got. Judging by the way she looks at him, it can't be anything all that important.*

"Are you off in a field thinking baseball

174

again?" Joanna demanded, breaking into Matt's thoughts.

"No, and just for that, I won't tell you what I *was* thinking about."

"Won't, hmm? It was baseball," Joanna said to Oliver complacently, nodding toward Matt.

"Changing the subject," Matt shot a defiant look at Joanna. "I found a boy at the park this week that can hit and pitch too, but he hasn't been back to play again."

Eleana smiled with the rest of them, not dreaming the boy was Juan.

"Funny thing," Matt said thoughtfully. "Maybe I've seen him somewhere before. He seems familiar somehow, something about him . . ."

Luke felt good going to work. His uniform was crisp and immaculate. But, he thought wryly, it always started out that way, before the humidity got hold of it. *I slept like I'd been hit on the head last night, too. That always helps. Now if my luck holds and somebody's got in early and made coffee —*

He smelled the coffee before he got to the end of the hall, and there was a sweet smell of cinnamon and sugar, and apple, too. He sniffed the delicious scents as he went in. There were some bakery boxes on the table.

Smells like a choice of apple-filled or cinna-mon sticks? He stifled a grin when his stomach growled.

Cooled off, sweet tooth satisfied, he fin-ished his coffee. Looking around for napkins he'd forgotten to get, Luke took the final bite of his apple-filled doughnut and licked his fingers. As he enjoyed the last of the sweet mess he glanced toward the door to see if he'd been caught doing such a child-ish thing. He got up and washed his sticky fingers, feeling ready to tackle his job.

He met a couple of the men and the receptionist on his way back to his office. He looked around again as he went in to see if Deputy Jack Kelly was waiting for him.

No sign of him yet. I'm early, though. And he will have to get his men lined out for the day.

While he waited, Luke pulled out a sheaf of papers to look at. They were held together by a jumbo paper clip. His usual pleasant expression gave way to a worried frown.

The reports of disappearances were add-ing up. More of them just this morning. *Of course, they may not really be disappear-ances . . .*

He ran through the reports, checking dates. The longest time missing was between two and three months. Some of the reports were fairly recent, and there were some inquiries about those already reported. *Just now getting desperate enough to call for help,* he decided about the new ones.

A knock interrupted his thoughts and he looked up to see Jack Kelly standing in the door.

"Jack, come in. I've been expecting you; I'm just wading through this current batch of troubles."

"I was afraid I'd surprised you. You got my message then?"

"Sure did. It always takes me a minute to get your name and your face together. How did that big difference happen, anyway, if you don't resent nosy questions?"

"No, I'm used to them." Jack's white teeth showed in a grin. "It was my grandmother's doing."

Jack sat down and got comfortable as he talked. "She thought since my father was a gringo, I should have a gringo name."

"And she didn't wait to see if you would have a gringo face to go with it?" Luke laughed.

"No. What can I say?" Jack laughed with him. "Somebody goofed?"

"No, nobody goofed. You're a good man by any name, and I've wished more than once that I could run you through the copy machine when we're short-handed. But what's on your mind? Is there something you could use a little help with?"

Serious at once, Jack got right to the point. "I've heard talk that there are inquiries coming in from relatives about men who are supposed to be working here in Las Flores but no one seems to know where they are."

"Yes." Luke was instantly alert. "Have you heard something that will shed some light on that?"

"I think so. And you're right, I need your help." Jack leaned forward a little. "One of my cousins has joined the missing list, and I think in looking for him, we may be able to find out about some more of the missing men."

"Your cousin is missing? When did you hear about this and how?" Luke held up his hand at the new wrinkle in Jack's forehead. "Just start at the beginning and tell me what you know."

Jack nodded, gathering his thoughts as he crossed his legs. He looked worried.

"My aunt called me last night and told me that my cousin José may be missing."

"May be missing. How long has he been gone and what makes her think he's missing instead of just out of pocket?"

"José comes up here every summer to work, then goes back home to go to school. He will go to the university next year," Jack said proudly.

Luke nodded his approval, waiting for more.

"He came up here to work like he always does, him and a friend of his. Then about a month ago — she said about two or three weeks at least — my aunt got a letter. Not from my cousin, José, but the friend he came with. My aunt hadn't heard from José, but thought he was just working and busy." Jack smiled briefly, "He's not much on correspondence. Anyway, they were supposed to work at the same place. He, the friend, told her that José had gone somewhere north of here to work for a Mr. Mansfield, but he didn't know where or the name of Mansfield's business. He hadn't heard from him and he was getting worried is why he wrote to his mother."

"Both families live in Mexico and the cousin and his friend came up here to work?"

"Yes." Jack went on looking grim. "My aunt checked around and no one else had heard anything from José either, and she didn't know where to turn so she called me and told me about it. You ever heard of this

Mansfield?"

"No, I haven't, Jack. But that at least gives us a name to work with. We've had zilch so far. *Nada.* The ones that had a friend with them seem to have taken the friend with them wherever it was they went." Luke shook his head. "A friend of my brother's asked me to see what I could find out about one of his friends. He had a friend with him, too, and they're both missing. The missing man's name is Carlos Castillo." He raised his eyebrows hopefully. "Ring any bells?"

"No, can't say it does," Jack said thoughtfully. "But when a friend goes, too, makes you think it must have been something good that they both wanted to take advantage of — like more money." Jack's eyes met Luke's.

Luke had a sudden thought. "Speaking of that, why didn't your cousin's friend go with him, Jack?"

"He is in *love,* Luke." Jack sat back and smiled slightly. "He was going home sooner than my cousin planned to."

"Oh. In love, hmm?" Luke's face turned solemn, thinking, *Love may have saved his life.* He didn't share that with Jack, who was already looking worried enough about his cousin. "What else did your aunt tell you?"

"That's about it. All Tía Sarita really knew was the man's name was Mansfield and the work was north of here. And the reason he went is that Mansfield promised to pay twice what they were getting where they were working."

"*Twice?* That's enough to make you suspicious right there." Luke frowned, narrowing his eyes.

"He either wanted them for some hurry-up job, or worse, he didn't intend to pay them after he got them where he was going. It's been done before. I know it's beginning to sound bad. I want to see if I can find this man, this Mansfield, if that's all we've got." Jack's face was as grim as Luke's. "José is my cousin. This is not just statistics anymore. It's family. I will go undercover if I have to."

Luke didn't answer immediately, then said, "Is your cousin's friend still here?"

"Yes, he is. He's still working right now as far as I know, but he will probably leave this weekend after he gets his pay."

"Get in touch with him and tell him we want to talk to him. No, wait." Luke shook his head, coming to a decision as he got up. "Better still, we'll go and talk to him right now. You do know where he's working?"

"Yes." Jack was glad Luke wanted to get started right away. "My car's in front. I'll drive."

In the car, Luke explained, "If I had a nickel for everyone that's run when we wanted to talk to them, I could retire early. If that boy's in love, he's not going to want to take any chances on any delays in getting home."

"Heck, I can understand that." Jack laughed, getting excited about finally making some progress. "You're older than I am, Luke."

"Yeah, and I hate to shock you, but I plan on getting a whole lot older, too."

They drove to a place with fields of produce in back of it, Luke noticing the generous wide areas in front paved to accommodate trucks. It was just off the main highway that ran through Las Flores. Jack pulled up at the rear of a produce warehouse with large, open sheds. From the car they looked over the men they could see working in the fields and in the sheds.

"Do you know him by sight? This friend of your cousin's?"

"Yes, but I don't see him. I'll have to ask for him. By the way, his name's Antonio. Friends call him Tony." Jack paused. "Do you want me to bring him out here?"

"Yes, I think that would be best. I'll wait here."

Jack got out and went to find the supervisor. Luke watched him go. From where he had parked, he was able to see the front side of the building as well as the back. The fields were flat, and it was easy to keep an eye open for anyone leaving the building.

Luke got out of the car when he saw Jack returning with Tony and held out his hand to the young man. They shook hands, and Luke introduced himself.

The boy spoke softly, said his name was Tony, and pronounced his last name carefully, though Luke didn't quite catch it. It was something that ended in an *o,* and Luke didn't want to make him any more nervous than he already was over a name Jack already knew. Luke just nodded, not moving any closer, and looking as friendly as his plain law officer's face could.

Tony, Luke noted, was a handsome young man. He was clean, honest looking, and met Luke's eyes even though he was a little nervous and wary. Luke chalked his anxiety up to his being worried about being able to leave for home soon.

Luke smiled to put him at ease and told him, "We want to talk to you about your friend who went to work for Mr. Mansfield. It was Mansfield, wasn't it?"

"José, you mean." He glanced at Jack. "Yes, sir." The young man nodded. "The man said his name was Mansfield, and he said he would pay us twice what we are getting here." Tony added as an afterthought, "I would have gone too, but I am going home after I get paid."

"Did he, this Mr. Mansfield, promise you anything else or just say that he would pay you twice what you were making? Did he tell you where his business was?"

"No." Tony shook his head, appearing unhappy that he couldn't tell Luke more about him. "I had never seen him or heard his name before. But I heard what Mansfield was telling people and I heard him tell someone else before I left that they made big crates —"

"Big crates? You mean wooden crates?"

"Yes, like the ones you send across the water with all your belongings in them. He said the work was not hard and there would be regular hours. I was on my way out and didn't hear very much more. He also said the work was north of here when someone else asked him."

"North of here?" Luke pricked up his ears. "Did he say how far north? Or say what it was near?"

"No, he only said all we had to do was put our names on the paper he had and go get on the bus."

"Bus. He had a bus?"

"Yes. It wasn't much of a bus, looked like an old school bus. One of the men asked where they would be going, and he said they would be there in about three hours. He didn't say the name of a town or anything about where it was, but I do remember he said three hours because I thought how I would hate to ride that old bus for three hours." Tony showed his white teeth in a smile at that.

Luke grinned back. "Yeah, I can understand that. Three hours, in this heat. Is there anything else you can think of that might tell us where they went?" Luke squinted against the sun, studying the boy as he spoke.

"No, I don't think of anything else. He never told us the name of the place or the name of his business. Just his name, Mansfield. And he said they made crates of all kinds, but are making the big ones now. I heard him tell José they are making the big ones is why they need a lot of men."

"Must have a government contract or something," Luke said to Jack. He turned back to Tony. "Did very many go with him?"

"I don't know. José said not to worry, that he might go with him, he hadn't decided yet. But I didn't see him again. No one has heard from José, or knows where the crate place is." Tony shifted his weight from one foot to the other. Luke could almost feel his concern about his friend; he didn't look at Jack but was sure he felt it, too.

"Was there a license plate on that bus?"

"Yes, and I looked at it as I left. It was all caked with mud, so I could not tell what it was." He stopped, his expression embarrassed because he didn't get the number or seemingly much else that would help them.

"I wish you'd been able to get that license plate, but it's not your fault you didn't get it. Mud is a cheap way to keep anyone from seeing a license number — it's done all the time."

Jack nodded encouragement, too, and Tony seemed to relax a bit.

"I — the men who were already standing by the bus to go with him," he continued thoughtfully, looking first at Luke and then at Jack, "they were the most poorly dressed of the ones we have seen looking around for work, and most of them didn't speak too much English." The young face was serious, thinking back to that day and the men he had seen. "They were talking among themselves in Spanish and looking around as if they might see police coming to question them any minute. Sort of watching, you know, as if they were afraid. I pointed this out to José. But it didn't make any difference to him. The money promised was good. I could see José had almost made up his mind to go. He must have gone, because I have not heard from him again."

"His family hasn't either. That's why we're looking for him," Luke explained.

"I am hoping to hear from him after I get home." This was said with an anxious glance at the supervisor, who was standing under one of the sheds watching them. "That is all I can tell you, sir."

"All right. Thank you for your help." Luke took a card out of his pocket. "If you think of anything else, call this number and ask for me or leave a message and I will call you back." He smiled, touching the boy's arm briefly. "Have a good trip home."

Back at the office Jack sat down as Luke took his place behind his desk. "Well, we know more than we did."

Luke pulled the phone book toward him and said, "Get that map over there and see what's about three hours north of here." He shrugged, "Of course, Mansfield may have lied about that, too."

As Jack studied the map, Luke looked in the yellow pages for crates, boxes, and whatever he could find under things related to carpentry and crates or something similar.

Jack moved his chair closer and put the map on Luke's desk. He looked up. "There are some little towns scattered around but nothing very big. And I can tell you first-hand, it's desolate country. Not much in the way of settlements or people. I think there are more Indians out there than other races, and some of the country is beautiful." He shook his head. "But you would really have to be a woods critter to appreciate it."

"Hey!" Luke had the phone book in his hand, looking excited. "Here's a crate place listed at a place called Glorianna. I've never heard of it, have you?"

"No, I haven't, but there it is." Jack stood up and peered with Luke at the map. "It's one of the tiny little towns I told you were scattered out there. What do you think?"

"I think we may have found our lying Mr. Mansfield. I hope lying is all he's guilty of." Luke's face looked hard as stone. "And you volunteered to go undercover. I'm taking you up on that."

Luke kept this missing-person assignment to himself and was Jack's contact. He stuck a memo to himself on a spindle to requisition other personnel and things they would need. His mind was already picturing the Texas Rangers he had requested before when he had a bust in mind. His first priority now was getting Jack what he needed for his undercover role.

Pushing everything else aside, Luke managed to get the clothes and equipment Jack didn't already have; pulled some strings to requisition a horse trailer and truck; borrowed a mule to go with all that; then drove Jack and his assorted gear two hours north toward Glorianna.

Out in the middle of nowhere, Luke pulled up by a small grove of trees and got out, checking the things he and Jack had gathered up for this trip.

Jack changed into the ragged, threadbare clothes and not-too-clean *serape* and wide hat he'd brought. His five-o'clock shadow was already a young beard that hid most of his bronze face. He'd forgone deodorant for a couple of days, and Luke commented he was beginning to smell right for the part he had to play.

"Right, or is it 'ripe'?" Jack quipped in spite of the heat.

"Ripe, I guess. But you look great." Luke sized him up. "And you'd better act like you don't know too much English —"

"You think I'll have trouble playing a wet-

189

back?" Jack gave him a pained expression.

"No, not a bit. The big town of Glorianna's about one hour that way." Luke pointed. "And since you don't know where the hell it is, you won't look suspicious by going right directly to the crate place." Luke was grinning from ear to ear as he regarded Jack and his undercover get-up.

"Just try not to enjoy this so much, amigo!" Jack checked to make sure he had his beaten-up canteen full. "By the time I get there, I'll look the part, all right."

"And now, your transportation," Luke said with a flourish as Jack made a swipe at him. He went around to the back of the trailer and led out a tired-looking mule with a brightly colored but dirty blanket on its back.

The little mule was old and stubborn, but small and surefooted, Luke had been assured. He watched as Jack got aboard the mule, which looked at him like he was a necessary evil. Jack looked down at the tough-looking little mule. He didn't seem any happier about the arrangement than the mule did.

"What's this?" Jack frowned at the mule, whose only sign of life was a listless flicking of one ear. "The Texas answer to Rent-A-Beast?"

"Well, you can't go undercover in a Mercedes," Luke pointed out, trying not to laugh.

"Yeah, tell me about it."

Without so much as a prod from Jack, the mule evidently decided it was time to go and began moving slowly, by some miracle, in the right direction. All Jack had to do was hang on.

"And Jack." Luke raised his voice. "Remember, you have two weeks. There is no way to check on you, no phone. You will be on your own for two weeks, then the Marines will land. The Texas Rangers and I will come down on Glorianna like a ton of bricks in two weeks. Mansfield is the only candidate for this, and he has that crate business, so he's got to be our man with the promises. With those men missing and no other information, we've got no choice but take a chance with the little information I've got."

The distance between Luke and Jack was slowly widening as Luke continued, "I will be there to make the bust, ready or not. Get all the evidence you can, but we will go over that place with a fine-toothed comb whether you've found anything or not."

Jack either nodded or the jolting mule made it look that way.

"Have a nice trip," Luke shouted after him.

Not looking back, Jack dug his heels into the mule's flanks.

"Giddyap, Mercedes!"

CHAPTER ELEVEN

Busy with her work, Eleana was startled by the sudden noise. She looked up to see the office manager rapping on a desk for attention.

"I've got an announcement to make. Everybody listen up!"

He looked around, waiting for one of the girls to get off the phone before he continued. "As was posted on the bulletin board yesterday, there will be an executive meeting this afternoon at three." He grinned. "The good news is, the rest of you can leave early. You can leave at five till three." Over a murmur of surprise and delight he added, "See you bright and early tomorrow morning."

Eleana exchanged excited comments with the others whose desks were close to hers.

"I'm going shopping," confided the one about Eleana's age. The older woman on the other side of Eleana said she was going home to bake cookies. Eleana's heart warmed to her, glancing at the pictures of her grandchildren, which flanked the calendar on her desk.

They looked expectantly at Eleana, who hadn't spoken.

"I don't know yet," she said slowly. "I think I might go out by the college, since I have heard about it and I haven't had a chance to see it yet."

She looked around. "Do any of you know if a bus goes out by there?"

"Oh, yes," the older woman assured her. "Most of the students who live here take the bus. Just ask the driver at the stop where you live, dear. He can tell you which one to take."

It didn't take Eleana long to walk back to her rooming house. Glad to have found a job she liked, she was also glad to have found a job she could walk to. She glanced up the familiar street. Coming in sight of her rooming house, she was also glad to see there was no one on the porch.

Señora Nosy must be busy in the kitchen. Perhaps she is baking as my friend at work is doing, though I have never smelled cookies there before.

Eleana hurried her steps. She went in quietly, not wanting to have to answer any

194

nosy questions. There was no one in the front part of the house.

She tiptoed up the stairs, pleased to have the extra time off, making plans.

I'll surprise Oliver. He mentioned he wanted me to see the college where he teaches, and I would like to go. What shall I wear?

Moving about her room quietly, she dressed in slacks and comfortable shoes. Satisfied with her choice and the becoming color she had chosen to impress Oliver, Eleana opened the door a bit to look down the stairs. There was not a sign of anyone. She did hear noises coming from the kitchen now, though there was no scent of anything baking or cooking.

"Perhaps she is cleaning," Eleana decided. She put the latch on the door and went quickly and quietly back down the stairs and outside without meeting or seeing anyone.

Feeling as if she was going to a secret rendezvous with all this stealth, Eleana looked back at the rooming house. She waved happily to one of the other roomers, who was looking out an upstairs window, and laughed to herself.

Now they can talk this afternoon about my coming home early and wonder where I might be going.

At the bus stop there was no one waiting but her. She was grateful for her unexpected holiday while everyone else in Las Flores was working. And in the distance she saw the bus coming. When it pulled to the curb, she stretched up on tiptoes to talk to the driver.

"Please, can you tell me where I can catch a bus that goes out to the college?"

The driver smiled. "You're about there now, ma'am. See those three people over there across the street?" He pointed and Eleana nodded.

"The bus they are waiting for will take you out to the college. There's a stop right in front of the college."

She thanked him and went across the street to wait with the others.

The ride was enjoyable and not as long as she expected. Eleana was the only one left on the bus by the time they reached the beginning of the school campus and the driver pointed it out to her. There were several buildings and wide lawns with walks crossing them. Eleana admired the well-kept campus.

When the bus stopped, Eleana got up and looked through the windshield across the expanse of lawn. "Do you know where the building is where art and painting is taught?"

"I'm not sure, miss," the driver said, looking uncertain. "But I think it's behind the buildings you see on this side. There's a garden and a small lake back there, and I think that's where it is."

Eleana thanked him and waited to cross the street, feeling nervous now that she had arrived. Walking toward the back of the campus, she admired the landscaping. It was farther than she thought it looked from the bus stop, and she looked around curiously at the buildings, admiring the flower beds and foundation plants.

The building she thought might be the one where painting was taught was low and wide and had a lot of windows. She went in, feeling like an intruder in the silent hall. She was looking around wondering which hallway to take when she heard footsteps coming toward her.

"Excuse me." She faced the approaching young man, who was obviously a student there. "Could you tell me, please, where Oliver Avery's classroom is?"

"Sure can." The young man smiled. "I'm going there. Come with me."

As they neared, Eleana saw the classroom door was open. Her heart fluttered, knowing Oliver was teaching his class there and he was not expecting her. She stopped, feeling strangely out of place.

Oliver looked up as the student came in, with Eleana following in the hall behind him. His face lit with such pleasure that Eleana felt better. He came to the door and took both her hands in his.

"Eleana! I'm glad you came. I wanted you to see where I work. Did you get off work early or something?"

"Yes, I —" Eleana stopped abruptly, her wide eyes looking over his shoulder in surprise.

In the center of the classroom was a large desk. On the desk sat a woman who was wearing a black mask with sunglasses and a shower cap and nothing else! The woman's body was well proportioned and beautiful, and she was posed in a relaxed and natural-looking lounging position that showed her natural beauty to good advantage as the students worked at their sketches of her.

Oliver turned to follow her gaze. "We're painting," Oliver explained. "Doing some sketches as well, from life today."

He nodded his head toward the woman. "She's a good model. Has a beautiful body, and can hold a pose for a long time without tiring."

"Yes, she is beautiful," Eleana acknowledged softly. Then, puzzled, she asked, "But, why is she wearing the mask and shower cap?"

Oliver took her hand and stepped out into the hall. He pulled the door shut behind him. "Because she lives here in Las Flores. The mask and the cap over her hair keep her from being recognized. She has a regular job, but with two small children to support, she needs the money. What she gets for modeling two afternoons here is as much as she gets all week at her other job."

Eleana listened, thinking about what it would be like to be stared at by all those eyes and be the subject of all those sketches.

Oliver stuck his head back in the door and beckoned to the student who had escorted Eleana to the class.

"I'm going down the hall for coffee. You're in charge. Come and get me if you need me." He added with a wink, "But please don't need me."

"I won't," the young man answered confidently. "The chocolate is better than the coffee," he said, smiling at Eleana.

Oliver and Eleana walked down to a recess in the hall, which held the drink machines. They had their choice of hot coffee and chocolate and an assortment of cold drinks. Oliver got coffee and Eleana chose hot chocolate.

"The coffee's not all that bad. A lot of my students just like chocolate better." Oliver made excuses for the brew in his hand. He turned to go back down the hall, holding his coffee in one hand and Eleana's hand in the other.

"There's a small break room, but I want to show you my office."

Two or three doors down from the classroom and on the other side of the hall, he stopped to unlock a door. Eleana was reminded that she always locked her room when she left the boardinghouse.

"I usually lock the door when I'm going to be in class or out for a long time."

Before Eleana could comment, he explained. "We don't have a burglary problem, nothing like that. But I keep my papers and grades in here. Besides which, absent-minded students borrow paints and brushes and then forget to return them. I like to know what's here to use when I want to do something."

She nodded her understanding, looking around with interest as she listened.

Oliver set his coffee on the desk, then took Eleana's chocolate and set it there, too.

"Do you know this is the first time we've ever had any time alone and away from prying eyes —"

"I guess that is true." Eleana remembered how she had slipped quietly out of her rooming house.

He pulled her to him, his arms going around her as his lips found hers. He kissed her long and tenderly, holding her close to him.

When he broke the kiss, they stood there cheek to cheek, arms linked, and when Oliver spoke, his voice was husky with emotion. "I — I care for you a lot, Eleana."

She stepped back a little, looking into his eyes. "I care for you too, Oliver." She said a little doubtfully, "But, you know, it hasn't been very long since we met in the mall. We do not know each other or our families, or even very much at all of each other," she reminded him.

"It seems long enough to me." Oliver grinned. "It doesn't take long when you meet the right one."

Someone knocked on the door and Oliver went to open it. He came back and said, "I've got to go back to class for a little while. If we didn't have the model, I could let them go early. But it won't be much longer now."

"I know you are working." She smiled proudly at him. "I will be all right, if I may wait here?"

"Of course, and I'll be back in" — he looked at his watch — "about twenty minutes. There's a restroom just off the break room down the hall where we got our coffee and chocolate. Make yourself at home."

I'll let the class go five or ten minutes early. What the heck? Oliver promised himself as he hurried back to his class.

Eleana walked around the office, admiring how neatly everything was put away, and looking with interest at some of Oliver's brushes and artist supplies.

When he returned, he stopped at the door and beckoned to her. "The students are leaving now. It doesn't take them long to clear out," he said with a laugh. "Come and I'll show you some of the sketches they've done, if you want to see them."

"Oh, yes, I would like to. I'm coming." She picked up her purse to follow him, pausing to toss her chocolate cup in a nearby trash can.

Some of the sketches he showed her were quite good, rating compliments.

"And I have a special one to show you." Oliver smiled mysteriously. "It's back in my office."

When they got there, Oliver went to a cabinet and took out a loosely rolled piece of sketching paper. Eleana felt an unexpected twinge of envy, thinking it might be one he had done of the beautiful model.

He carefully unrolled it and held it up for her to admire. "Do you like it?"

It was the sketch he had done of her the first time he had seen her in the mall.

"*Oliver!* Did you do this?" She was delighted with the sketch.

"Yes. The first time I saw you I knew I had to find those Spanish eyes again. I saw you standing on the mezzanine above me when I came into the mall. And you were looking down, not even seeing me or the other unimportant people because you were looking for someone else."

"Yes, yes I *did* see you," Eleana protested. "I didn't want to stare. I could not tell you who any of those other people were, but I saw you, Oliver. I called you the Golden One because of the way your hair caught the bright sun from the skylight above us. It made your hair look golden."

Oliver was amused at her fascination with mere sun streaks but was pleased she had noticed him. She held the sketch carefully, still admiring it.

"You can keep it, if you would like to." He smiled. "I'm glad you like it."

"Yes, I would like to keep it. Please, roll it

up as you had it so I can carry it without hurting it."

"Hurting it?" Oliver laughed. "It is not alive, Eleana, only a likeness. And I couldn't let it go unless I had the original." He put his arms around her, kissing her again.

Eleana was pleased with the sketch, planning to show it to Carlotta as soon as she could, to show her how talented Oliver was. She held it carefully as Oliver locked the office door, then checked to make sure the classroom door was locked as they left.

As they walked toward the parking lot he commented, "I'm glad you're wearing slacks. Matt is having a game at six o'clock, and I told him we'd try to get out there and see as much of it as possible. I didn't know you would have this time off."

"I didn't know either. I did know there was a meeting scheduled this afternoon, but they surprised us with the time off. And I wanted to see the college, where you teach."

"Good luck for us," he said, smiling. "We can go on out to the game now, then all of us can go somewhere and eat after that, if that's all right with you."

"Yes, I would like to go. Matt enjoys baseball so, and now I will get to see a whole game."

They were early getting to the park, and

Oliver showed her around, pointing out the pavilions for picnics, a sunken garden with benches, and the place that was roped off for swimming.

Eleana stood gazing at the area for swimming. She knew this must be the place Juan told her about. It was a beautiful location, and he could easily come to swim and watch games when he wasn't working, since it was within walking distance of the clinic and the convent.

She smiled at Oliver. "It's nice, a good place for the children to swim."

By the time they got back to the field, there were already quite a few people there and Matt was warming up with his players. Joanna stood briefly and waved to them. They went to sit with her.

At a distance, Matt had stopped and pointed. A boy started in the direction he had pointed; no words were needed for Matt to get his point across. Eleana turned to look at the newcomer Matt had summoned, and her heart skipped a beat.

It's Juan!

As she watched, Matt clapped Juan's shoulder as if he were glad to see him and was busily giving him instructions of some sort. Eleana was glad she was as far away as she was. She feared that if Juan saw her, they would give themselves away. She sat on the far side of Joanna and Oliver, not looking directly at Juan.

It had taken such a shock to remind her how precariously she was balanced between two different worlds. She walked a dangerous tightrope between her everyday life and her relationship with Oliver, and the problems of Carlotta and Juan, which threatened to come between them.

The boys playing ball were too engrossed in their game to pay any attention to the spectators. Eleana was sure Juan had not seen her. After the game, as Matt talked to his teams, Eleana asked Oliver to show her more of the sunken garden as an excuse to get away before Matt let the players go.

Oliver took her hand, glad to have the opportunity for another kiss. She turned and started walking away as Oliver turned to call to Matt.

"We'll wait for you in the parking lot."

Safely away from most of the crowd and the teams, Oliver got his kiss, and Eleana quickly noted the garden and the parking lot were not near the route Juan would probably take when he went back to the convent.

At dinner that evening, Matt bragged about the way his boys played and speculated on which ones he could use when school started.

Uneasy, Eleana changed the subject by asking Joanna where she was going to have her baby, her little Matt or Joanna.

Joanna was glad to have someone to talk to about their plans. "As soon as I know I am pregnant, I'm going to the clinic by the convent, Los Niños, it's called."

Joanna talked happily, not noticing Eleana's silence. "It's a good thing we have insurance. Without it, I don't think Matt and I could afford a broken bone, much less a baby."

"You'd think the school system could afford benefits with what they save on the salary they pay," Matt's sarcasm informed them.

"The way you like baseball, it's a wonder they don't charge you to let you coach," Oliver teased him.

Baseball didn't interest Eleana, but what Joanna said about the clinic did. "It must cost a lot then, to have a baby at the clinic?" Eleana's dark eyes looked worried.

Joanna nodded. "There's the room of course, and the delivery room where you have the baby, and the anesthesia and all sorts of things. And all that is besides the doctor's bill. Yes, it costs a lot, all right. But since we have insurance, we won't have to pay but a small part of it."

Thoughts of all the things they would need when Carlotta had her baby came to haunt Eleana. *Carlotta's dream was to have her baby here, and now she is at the clinic. She is safe there, but my poor Carlotta, she doesn't know how much all this is going to cost!*

Her preoccupation with Carlotta and her baby kept her from hearing much more of the conversation around her.

Carlotta has her salary and she has been saving the money from the sewing she has done, but that is all she has. And we have not heard anything from Carlos. Oh . . . Eleana's heart sank into misery she had no way to control.

Her troubled thoughts kept her from contributing any more to the conversation. She had nearly shredded the paper napkin in her lap by the time they left.

"A penny for your thoughts." Oliver kissed her forehead as he held the car door for her.

"I — I don't think that would cover them," she said, not realizing how sad she sounded.

Oliver laughed, thinking she was joking. "Expensive ideas, are they? Well, you obviously have good taste — you're with me."

Eleana smiled up at him, her heart heavy, wishing she could confide in him, afraid of what he would think if she did.

When they said goodnight and Oliver drove her home, he stopped a little way down the block in front of a vacant lot. There were trees and shadows there, and it was quite a way from the streetlight.

"I don't know why I didn't think of this before." Oliver was pleased with himself. "I can kiss you goodnight here and then walk you up to your front door."

"Oliver, I want to ask you something."

"All right, what is it?"

"The model. The one at the college. You said she made more modeling than on her regular job." Eleana hung her head, not meeting his eyes. "Do you think I could be a model, Oliver?"

"You?" His brows drew together in a frown. "I don't know." His voice was unbelieving, "Would you *want* to?"

"Yes," she drew a deep breath. "I — I think so."

"But, why? If you need money I will loan you some, or help you any way I can."

"No. I make enough at my job," she said and shifted uncomfortably, knowing the only explanation she could offer was weak. "It is — for someone else."

"Someone else? Who? Who else would you need to help that much?" Anger made Oliver's demand sound harsh.

She looked down again, studying the cracked concrete beneath their feet. It looked like a chasm between her and the man she loved. "I'm sorry, Oliver. I cannot tell you."

Oliver's temperature was rising, and his eyes were angry. "We've been through this before." His voice was nearly a growl. "It's got something to do with that message and those mysterious visits, hasn't it?"

There was no answer.

"Hasn't it?"

Wordlessly, without looking up, Eleana nodded.

Oliver stood waiting until it was obvious he would learn nothing else.

"All right," he finally conceded. "I'll check into it for you, about modeling, and let you know." His voice was cold as he moved away from her.

Oliver walked her to the rooming house, but he did not kiss her goodnight.

Eleana nodded to the landlady, who still sat on the porch fanning herself. Her eyes studied each of them, but neither looked at her.

Oliver held the door for Eleana, then he

abruptly turned and strode quickly down the steps. Eleana could still feel his anger, without looking back to see the way he hurried to his car. Her heart ached as though each step he took away from her was on its broken pieces, grinding them into the cracked concrete.

For Eleana, the night was filled with nightmares. She dreamed of Carlotta's shocked face when she learned how much she owed the clinic, and unseen demons in white were reaching for her baby. They were taking her firstborn to pay the clinic, like some fairy tale peopled with ogres and other horrors. Her nightmare imagination showed her Carlos and Jorge's broken bodies, their eyes open and in pain or empty and dead in some desolate and undiscovered place. She dreamed, too, of Carlotta and Juan's dangerous journey to the convent. She saw them running blindly from patrols, from their dogs and falling down, falling, falling —

Eleana woke with a start. She sat up, in a cold sweat from fright. Then her misery doubled because she remembered that Oliver was angry with her. And the latest reason Oliver was angry with her made her blush in the dark.

She thought of the woman sitting naked

on the desk at the college and felt like a fallen woman. Lonely and ashamed, salty tears soaked into her pillow as she fell back into an exhausted sleep.

CHAPTER TWELVE

Parker glanced in at the men working and strolled over to the man he had left in charge.

"Looks like we're doing pretty well getting the crates out. We'll probably be finished before the promised time. What do you think?"

"Yeah, I think we will too, at the rate we're going." The helper looked around at the dirty, ragged men who worked like zombies without expression and without talking to each other except for the little communication necessary to their jobs.

"These poor devils don't look like much, but they can sure turn out the work."

He turned slightly and gave Parker an intense look, obviously deciding to speak up on something he deemed important. "You should tell Mansfield to feed them better. It would pay in the long run, to keep them healthy." He stopped when he got it said, not taking his eyes off Parker.

He figured Parker would kill him without batting an eye if he knew what he thought of him, and he was right. He was as much a prisoner as the poor wretches he had to watch over until the job was done.

"We're not interested in the long run, just the long *green*." Parker chuckled at his own wit, pleased with himself.

No other suggestions were given. The temporarily-in-charge manager knew there was no sense wasting breath on any suggestions for improvement in the laborers' working conditions. There would not be any change, except for the worse for him personally, if he didn't watch what he said.

The erstwhile superintendent walked away a short distance, pretending to watch the side of a crate being nailed. After looking around a little more, Parker turned to go.

Remembering something at the last minute, Parker stopped and called back. He pointed to Carlos and Jorge. "See those two over there?" He spoke just loud enough for the other man to hear him.

The superintendent looked at Carlos and Jorge, who were working together on a nearby crate. He nodded, "Carlos and Jorge? Two of my best workers. They came together, work together good. What about them?"

"Just before time to knock off, tell them Mansfield will see them, and let them go about half an hour early."

"Okay, I'll tell them." He stood watching Parker swagger out, wondering what new meanness he was up to now. It wasn't good, Mansfield seeing Carlos and Jorge, he was sure of that.

The supervisor spat tobacco juice on the floor, worried. *Wonder what the problem is? There's got to be one for Mansfield to see them. If they ain't got a problem now, they will have when they get to Mansfield.* His eyes strayed back to Carlos and Jorge, hoping they would not be the next ones to disappear. A sudden chill made him shiver as he turned away, helpless to do anything about that. All he could do was give them the message as Parker had told him to.

When it was closer to quitting time, Jorge and Carlos looked at each other in surprise when they were told they could leave half an hour early.

"Wrap up what you're working on before you leave. Mansfield wants to see you," is all they were told.

Jorge wiped his hands on his dirty shirt. "We asked to see him twice and it's been

215

over a week since the last time we asked to see him, Carlos. I thought he would just forget about us."

Carlos shook his head. "We never know what to expect from him except that whatever the problem is, when he's asked about it, the problem always gets worse somehow. But, we didn't mention any complaint or say anything except that we want to talk to him."

Thinking back over the message, Carlos didn't look any happier than Jorge at the news Mansfield would see them. "As I said from the beginning, I don't trust him. There is one bad *hombre.* One thing I am sure of, he is seeing us because we asked twice. Or if not that, it is either something good for him or bad for us — both, if he can fix it that way." Carlos nervously tried to wipe his hands too. Nothing but sweat came off. He looked with distaste at his grimy palms.

"After this, every time I take a bath, I will thank the good Lord," he muttered to himself as he straightened his clothes the best he could.

At the time he was told to, the supervisor beckoned to Carlos and Jorge. He pointed toward the door and they obediently left their work. No one seemed to pay them any attention as they left. Too tired to make any more guesses, Jorge simply nodded to Carlos. They walked out together and went toward Mansfield's office.

The office door was open. Mansfield saw them coming. He quickly waved them to a couple of chairs on the other side of the small office as they entered.

I guess we must smell pretty bad, Carlos thought as he sat down and looked across the room at Mansfield.

Jorge was glad to see that Parker wasn't there. "That man is a devil," he had whispered to Carlos as they approached Mansfield's office. "He likes to hurt people, likes to see them suffering."

Both of them sat quietly, looking at the floor in front of them, waiting for Mansfield to speak. Their leg muscles finally relaxed a little; it was as if they didn't know how to sit, had forgotten anything but work and lying horizontal in an exhausted sleep.

"I got word you two wanted to talk to me." Mansfield raised his eyebrows inquiringly.

Carlos looked up and nodded respectfully. "Yes, we would like to ask you about some things."

"Such as?" His attitude said, "What more can you ask, free food and lodging —"

"When we agreed to come here and work

for you, Mr. Mansfield, you promised us twice as much money as we are getting. Then you said there had been a robbery somewhere?"

"Yes, took the whole payroll, the bastards did. But you have been getting paid every week. I have personally seen to that." Mansfield looked proud of himself and as close to noble as he could get without laughing.

"Yes, we have been getting paid. But we have not been getting the pay that we were promised."

Jorge chimed in to help Carlos. "And the food. It does not agree with us sometimes and we are sick. And there is no place for us to wash ourselves." Absentmindedly, he scratched as he talked.

Mansfield chuckled, watching Jorge scratch. "Yeah," he admitted. "The plumbing and the well pump are old and sort of . . . temperamental, I guess you could say. But we do manage to get you enough water to bathe once a week. That's about the best we can do right now."

He drew on his cigar, regarding Jorge and Carlos through the smoke.

"Mr. Mansfield." Carlos sat on the edge of his chair. "We have waited long enough for our money. And conditions here are worse than any I have ever seen anywhere."

218

Jorge nodded, backing Carlos up, trying not to scratch again.

"So?" Mansfield slouched in his chair, narrowing his eyes at them as if daring them to say more.

"So we want our money, and we want it now. Or as soon as you can manage to get it for us. We will be leaving to go home soon. My wife is expecting a baby, and the little one, it is due now. I need to go home to be with her."

"Well, we'll be sorry to lose you. The supervisor on your shift says you are both good workers, but I'm afraid there's nothing I can do about the money. When the home office found out how well they could do with half what they were paying, they cut the salary in half. Sorry, boys. You know how these company efficiency experts are." He grinned at them.

Carlos got up, outraged at how helpless they were. If he weren't so weak, he would have dashed across the room and hit Mansfield. Wiped the hateful, self-satisfied grin off his face.

"You mean you are not going to give us the money you promised?"

"No. You're getting as much as you were when we found you. Take it or leave it." Mansfield's voice was flat and final as a marble slab.

"We will report you." Jorge stood up too. "You lied about the pay. And I know that must be against the law. And conditions like this! You are out here where no one can see what you are doing. But, *we will report you.*" Jorge's clenched fists and the expression on his face made it a solemn promise.

Carlos nodded agreement, but he saw something scary in Mansfield's eyes at the threat. He put his hand on Jorge's arm.

"Never mind, Jorge."

He looked at Mansfield. "If no one else punishes you, God will. We will leave in the morning. Will you ask Parker to take us back, at least to within walking distance to Las Flores?"

Mansfield looked speculative, then gave a brief nod. "Sure. No problem. Be ready to leave first thing in the morning."

At least when they left, they felt relief that they would be leaving in the morning.

Safely out of the office, Carlos and Jorge talked softly on the way back.

"I had the feeling all the time that we would not get our money. He lied to us about the robbery and all the other things. All of it was lies to get us here, that is all. And I think it is a good thing we went through that pretense of burying our money

220

in a can out behind the pump."

Carlos looked around carefully before he felt around the top of his pants and the places in his shirt where he had sewn his money.

"Yes, I saw Parker. He thought he was hidden, but I saw him watching us bury the can."

"At least this way, we always had our money with us."

Having checked their money, they fell silent for a few seconds, thinking of leaving.

"And we will report him, won't we, Carlos? I know this must be against the law. And the ones who disappeared, what of them?" The whites of Jorge's eyes showed large in the dimming light. "And what of the one I found in the shallow grave?"

Carlos nodded grimly. "Of course we will report him and what he is doing here. But I saw his face when you told him that. How he looked when you said we would report him. And he would deny it, Jorge. Or kill us if he had to, to shut us up. He has killed others for only complaining. He may have a phony smile, but he is as evil as Parker."

They were now meeting men coming from the work area. It was too late to go back to work. They turned and joined the men lining up to get their evening meal. They ate in silence, slowly, trying to select the parts of the food they didn't think would make them sick. The stringy meat they didn't touch, but the stale bread they did eat. They ate the beans and what they thought from the scent of it was some kind of cabbage. They were bone tired as they went to their sleeping mats, too exhausted to worry about how filthy they were.

"I will be glad to be home again," Jorge said softly as he lay down beside Carlos. "We had better sleep while we can. Parker may not take us far, and we will have a long, hot walk back to Las Flores."

Though the ground was hard, they were tired enough to sleep soundly, both glad to their bones they would be leaving this awful place in the morning.

Sister Rosa joined Mother Clare on the patio for a cup of coffee and to talk a little while before they went back to their duties.

"I haven't seen Carlotta too often. She is all right, isn't she? It must be getting near time for her baby."

"Yes, it's due any time now. But it will come when the Lord allows. She is healthy and takes care of herself and Juan too. I think it is a very good thing she is here at the clinic."

"You are right, but all we could do is give them a place to sleep, officially, you know." Mother Clare's angelic face took on a worried look. "I hope everything will be all right for them. But the baby will be born here. That is her main concern."

"We must pray for the little family."

Mother Clare tilted her head, wondering what she meant, since her expression was so serious.

"Juan told me that the father, Carlotta's husband, is here working somewhere. He has papers that are in order, but they do not know where he is. Juan's sister has told him this. He asked me to pray for his brother."

"Oh." Mother Clare clasped her hands in distress. "He is missing?"

"They do not think he is missing," Sister Rosa said quickly. "It is only that he must have taken a different job somewhere without telling them. Perhaps he had no chance to tell them. And Carlotta does not seem worried. She says Carlos should be home any day now."

"I hope she is right. And you are right, we will pray for them." She studied Sister Rosa. "But you are worried, aren't you?"

"Yes. It is not like a family this close not to keep in touch with each other. I wonder about that. And I think in the back of her mind, Carlotta is worried too." She sighed. "I cannot speak to her of it, of course, but I fear her husband doesn't know she has come here and that is another cause for worry. I hope she will hear from him soon and everything will be all right."

"I hope so too. Who is to deliver her baby?"

"Dr. Estival. He will not take any money for it. Stanley could find no way to put her on the clinic's insurance, so he is not charging for the hospital stay or anything, and there will be no charge from Dr. Estival. He may have to charge for whatever supplies they use, and, of course, the needed medication."

"That is a blessing. She will have enough for that. I hear she is doing quite well with the sewing that comes to the store." This brought a smile. "And the customers are pleased to have this service."

"Who is the pretty visitor who came to see her, do you know?"

"Yes, that is Juan's sister, the one I told you about. She is Carlotta's sister-in-law. She works in Las Flores." Her face lit with affection at the mention of Juan. "Juan adores her. He runs to meet her when she comes and hugs her as if she is Saint Nicholas come early!" Sister Rosa laughed.

Mother Clare smiled. "It is indeed strange that a family who stays so close should lose touch, even for a little while, of a father. And the father is Juan's brother?"

"Yes. His name is Carlos. We will pray about it, surely they will hear from him soon."

But the baby couldn't wait any longer for a tardy father. He considered nothing but his own readiness. And he was ready.

Fortunately, Carlotta was working with one of the nurses when her water broke, and they lost no time in taking charge of her and locating Juan and Sister Rosa.

It was the middle of the afternoon on a weekday, when everyone was working, not that it made any difference to him. Little Carlos Enrique Miguel DeRosa Castillo made his presence known in this world with a loud and lusty wail.

Sister Rosa and Juan held Carlotta's hand and told her how beautiful he was, then Juan ran to call Eleana at work.

"Oh!" Eleana gasped when Juan blurted out his good news. She could hardly contain her excitement, and the others near her desk turned curious looks on her as she talked. She smiled assurances at them, talking to Juan in Spanish.

"I will be there as soon as I get off from work," she assured Juan. "And how is Carlotta? She and the baby are well, everything is all right, and he is a fine healthy boy?"

"Carlotta is fine, Eleana. The baby is fine. And I, I am *Tío Juan!*"

Eleana laughed, dashing away a tear. "Tell her I am coming!"

She turned to explain to her listening friends, "My sister-in-law, my brother's wife, she has had her baby. He is a fine boy and they are both doing well."

After all the congratulations she went back to her work. But her worried look returned when she remembered she was to see Oliver that night.

She had seen Oliver twice since he got angry with her, but they had not seemed as close, and he had not kissed her again like he had at the school that day. Her heart ached as she remembered the kiss and his arms around her.

Oh, Oliver, I wish I could tell you. And I will. I will tell you as soon as I can.

She knew he might call her soon about the modeling job. He had promised he would call the next time they had a class that would sketch from real life. She cringed at "real life," dreading what she had decided to do.

He will call, because he promised. He is a good man, but he is angry, and I don't blame him. No, I do not blame him. But I love him so, and I miss him. Oh, Oliver, if only I could tell you. Her lip trembled and she kept her head down, concentrating on her work, trying not to think of Oliver's angry face or his warm arms or her aching heart.

CHAPTER THIRTEEN

This time when Oliver got the frustrating message that Eleana had had to leave, he managed to show so little emotion he was actually proud of himself. At least that's what he tried to think. The truth was he was already wounded as deeply as he could be and still have any contact at all with Eleana.

What is this all about, and where could she have gone? And why won't she tell me what's going on?

Eleana tried not to think of Oliver's reaction to her being called away again. She telephoned to leave him a message with her landlady and went directly from work to the clinic. There being no way to make peace with Oliver, she only prayed she would soon be able to tell him her problems. But she could not help that now. She stayed with Carlotta until visiting hours were nearly over, knowing she would have to leave to catch the last bus home.

"Tío Juan," Eleana murmured, looking fondly at him. A smile brightened her face at the title. "By the way, Juan, I saw you play ball at the park. And you played well, too. I am proud of you."

"I only played when they sent for me," Juan hastily explained. "And I told no one my name. And always, when I go to watch or play, I leave before anyone can start asking me questions about my name or where I live."

"I know you do, Juan. And I left a little early when I saw you that day. I was afraid we would give ourselves away if we suddenly met like that, not knowing the other was there. But Matt is a friend of my friend Oliver."

Juan's face was one big smile that curved his lips upward and sparkled in his eyes when he said Matt's name. "I know, and I am glad you told me. Eleana, I like Matt. He is a good *hombre* and there is nothing, *nothing* he does not know about baseball!" Juan's eyes glowed with admiration.

"I know he talks about baseball every time we are with him." Eleana smiled, remembering how Joanna teased him about baseball. "I wanted to warn you we might be at a game where you are playing some time."

"Yes, I am glad you told me." He glanced at Carlotta, getting serious again. "But, we may be going home soon."

Eleana looked up at the clock; it was nearly time for the last bus. She bent to give Carlotta a hug and kissed her forehead as she said goodbye.

Juan went out to the bus stop with her. Her heart warmed to her young escort as he walked beside her. *Tío Juan.*

Looking down the street for the bus, Juan asked, "You still have not heard anything from Carlos?"

"No. Nor has Raquel. But Jorge is with him. I am sure we will hear something soon." Eleana sounded more certain than she felt, trying to cheer him.

The approach of the bus cut off any more speculation about where Carlos and Jorge were. Eleana kissed Juan's cheek as the bus pulled to the curb.

She watched lights coming on in houses along the way as she rode home and thought of Oliver.

He was already angry with me when I sent this last message that I had to leave. He might not ever give me a chance to explain. A tear escaped and rolled down her cheek in spite of her, and another threatened to follow. She wondered if she had lost him forever.

The scenery passed the bus windows unnoticed in the anonymous dark. Eleana sat still as the night, her eyes sad and unseeing. She only noticed how the streetlights made little puddles of light at the corners of the streets. How lonely they looked in the dusk of the evening. The bus stopped and she walked with measured tread toward the rooming house.

Her pace was slow and sad, as if she were bone weary. As she passed the big tree across the street, her eyes wandered to its darker shade where Oliver had waited for her that first night she had been called away. But there was no car, nothing moved. Oliver was not there.

Parker had been watching and saw Carlos and Jorge leave Mansfield's office. As soon as they had gone around the building, he made his way to the door and looked in.

Mansfield called to him. "Come in. We need to talk."

Parker went in and hitched his chair closer to the desk, watching Mansfield's expression. He was pretty sure of what was coming.

"I thought we would. Those two are asking for trouble, right?" He grinned in anticipation. Parker considered himself the

Vice President of Trouble Prevention.

Mansfield put on a hurt expression. "They don't think much of our conditions here."

Parker raised his eyebrows, a comically incredulous expression on his face. "Pshaw! You don't say. But then . . ." He gave an exaggerated shrug. "You can tell by looking at them that they're used to the best." His fat jowls wobbled as he slapped his knee, laughing. His eyes were mere slits of evil mirth.

"Not only that, Parker, my man," Mansfield continued. "They are threatening to 'report us to the authorities.' Now, what do you think of *that?*"

"They're in no position to report anything," Parker spat contemptuously. "But I'll give them some authority to report to, you can count on that. What they'd get in Las Flores would be a quick bus ride back to Mexico if they open their mouths."

"But these upstanding gentlemen have papers, Parker, *papers.*" Mansfield shot Parker a serious look. "Be sure to take care of those papers before they, shall we say, *leave our hospitality.*"

"I always do, boss, always do. And the money they have, I get all of that, don't I? Like always?" He grinned again, "I know where they hid it."

"What money?" Mansfield's face was bland as he blew out a lazy puff of smoke.

"Yeah, yeah. What was I thinking? What money?" He stifled a high-pitched cackle, looking smug.

Mansfield sat contemplating his desktop. Parker let his chair legs down with a loud thump, impatient, "When do you want me to do it, boss? Tonight?"

"No. No need. I told them to be ready to leave first thing in the morning." He squinted up at Parker. "They said they want a ride to within walking distance of Las Flores."

"They do, do they? Walking distance, huh?" Parker laughed again, getting up. "Damn! I almost hate to see them go. They've been good for a lot of laughs."

"Yeah. Well, we can just afford so much amusement. Remember now," Mansfield said, getting serious. "No identification, or anything else that might tie us to them. I don't guess I need to tell you that having money on them if they are found anywhere, even later on, is a giveaway that they've been working somewhere?"

"No. I'm good at taking care of that. And these saps have their money buried in a can. Can you beat that? I've been watching them. These saps always wrap their stash in something or put it in a can. These two are of the can persuasion. What I'll do is not let them get it, think they can come back for it after they've reported us and the conditions here. And don't worry," Parker promised through his teeth, "I'll take those papers off them, too."

"Good, see that you do. If their bodies ever wash up or are found, there will be no identification." His eyes warned Parker. "Nor any indications of foul play." He got up as Parker turned and walked to the office door with him.

"They'll be ready in the morning. I guess you're going to be way ahead of them if you want to get them before they have a chance to dig up that can?" Mansfield grinned, picturing it.

"I'll see to it, boss."

Mansfield watched him swagger away, knowing he'd not only do a thorough job, he'd enjoy it.

"What?" Carlos rubbed his eyes, looking around the next morning.

Parker had wakened him and was now prodding Jorge with the toe of his boot.

"Up and at it!" Parker kept his voice down. "Get a move on if you want to go with me. I'm ready to go, and I don't intend

234

to wait around."

Carlos and Jorge had slept in their clothes and had no belongings left to gather up. With a glance at Parker, Carlos touched Jorge's arm and said, "We need to go out behind the building a minute."

"Okay, I'll go with you." Parker was not about to give them a chance to get to their money.

Jorge pretended to look disappointed and Carlos kept up the pretense, hesitating a bit.

"Later," Carlos whispered just loud enough to be heard. Parker smiled to himself, not looking back as he led the way.

There was nothing to keep them. Carlos and Jorge took a last look back, and Parker had them in his jeep before any of the rest of the men began waking up. A weak, pale dawn was just getting light enough to see.

"At least it is cooler to be going now," Jorge observed.

Carlos nodded, again glancing back at the low buildings. A scared feeling fluttered around his insides as he wondered where the shallow grave was that Jorge had found. The notion of that grave nearly overwhelmed the glad feeling Carlos had about leaving. He fought all the bad thoughts with memories of Carlotta and home.

Parker didn't bother making any conversation. His mind was busy deciding on a suitable place for the job before him. These men were half starved and weak, but more determined than the others they usually had to deal with.

Thinking over the route he was taking, he decided to drive them to the cliff above the river where the water was deepest. If the fall didn't finish them, the current and the rocks would.

Having made up his mind, Parker picked up speed. Carlos noticed it and shot a worried look at Jorge.

Jorge was worried, too. He looked out the windows at the desolate land around them and at the back of Parker's head. Pretending to scratch, he fingered the bills sewn behind the pocket of his shirt. He remembered how Parker had laughed at the paper Carlos had with the needle and thread wrapped in it.

That was before we knew we had more than rips and holes to sew up.

Carlos too was gazing at the back of Parker's head as he drove. *He is not even pretending to talk to us. I wonder how far he is going to take us? He is one mean* hombre, *that one. He would not be giving us this ride if he had not been ordered to.*

Moving nothing but his eyes, Carlos looked around in vain for anything that could be used for a weapon. He felt a tingle of fear when he realized there was nothing at all. He thought of the gun Parker always carried.

Parker glanced in his mirrors at the road behind him. They were approaching the place he had decided would suit the business at hand. There was nothing moving for miles except them. He slowed down, pulling off the road.

Carlos and Jorge looked around too, wondering, fearing, why he had stopped here.

"Nature's calling. You boys might as well get out, too, and stretch," Parker said. He opened the back door.

Carlos and Jorge got out slowly, watching, still fearfully looking over the deserted area. Then Parker was motioning them forward.

Parker walked behind them, with them more than an arm's length ahead. Then he abruptly ordered them to stop and look down.

They were almost at the edge of a high ridge and could see a long way down a valley and across to other rocky canyon walls. Far below them a river ran, lush underbrush and trees making it a beautiful scene.

"See if you boys can hit the water." Parker laughed, enjoying himself.

Insulted, shocked at his vulgarity, Carlos glared at him. Then he gasped, realizing Parker didn't mean with a stream of urine, he meant for them to jump!

"I don't need to —" Jorge had started, and began to move back, away from the edge.

"Oh, but you *do* need to!" Parker was grim now. He stopped waving his gun around and leveled it at them. It looked like a deadly cannon to them. They both stopped, staring at the barrel, hardly daring to breathe.

"What? What are you going to do?" Jorge asked fearfully.

"I'm not going to do a thing. *You* are." Parker took a menacing step forward, closing in on them, his gun leveled.

Jorge wheeled around, but he was closer to the edge than he thought he was. His eyes wide and frightened, he teetered dangerously. Carlos leaped the few feet between them and grabbed Jorge's arm.

"You cannot do this!" he yelled at Parker.

"Why not?" Parker sneered. "You think anybody's going to miss a couple of illegal aliens?"

"We are here legally," Carlos told him, trying to think of some defense, hanging onto Jorge.

"Oh, is that so? You have papers? Let me see them," Parker demanded.

Still holding to Jorge's arm at the edge, where he'd frozen in panic, Carlos pulled the folded papers from his pocket with his other hand and handed them to Parker.

Parker took them, looked at them briefly, and stuck them in his pocket. "And you?" He waved his gun at Jorge.

Jorge just breathed noisily, not moving. Carlos managed to get his papers out of his pocket. He handed them to Parker, standing still, not daring to look back past Jorge.

Jorge knew what a useless thing this was, to show Parker papers or anything else. His only reality was Carlos holding onto his arm as he stared down at certain death. His desperate eyes moved, searched the barren ground at their feet for anything to use to defend themselves.

Parker calmly put their papers into his pocket without looking at them or commenting. Instead, he asked "Any driver's license or any other identification you got on you?" His words hit them like bullets.

"Identification?" Jorge spoke then. He knew he was a dead man. His arm under

Carlos's hand was cold. Parker raised his gun.

The grip Carlos had on Jorge's arm tightened as Jorge tried to take a step back and stumbled.

Carlos jumped to seize Jorge firmly with both hands as Parker's gun fired a warning shot. Carlos felt a searing pain in his shoulder as they fell. The fall from that height was like a nightmare in slow motion. The wind swirled around them. Carlos and Jorge were flying from the ridge, like wounded eagles, toward the water below.

Parker watched for several minutes, saw them hit the water and disappear. They didn't come up. He saw no signs of life in the swift-moving water. It was rocky where the two had disappeared; a ridge of rocks stuck up like prehistoric fossil teeth from the fast-flowing water. He gave a grunt of satisfaction. Carlos and Jorge had disappeared into a watery grave and probably would not ever be found.

Parker holstered his gun and put the papers in the jeep. He returned and watched the water a few minutes, but there was no sign of Carlos or Jorge. His job was done.

Getting comfortable in the jeep, he looked over Carlos and Jorge's identification and carefully put the papers he had demanded of them in the glove compartment to give to Mansfield. A proof he'd finished the job. He turned the jeep around and started back to report.

He had to wait to do any bragging. When he got back, Mansfield was talking to some man about working for him. Parker was standing near the door waiting when Mansfield appeared with a man he had never seen before.

"Ah! Here is Mr. Parker." Mansfield beamed, his broad smile at its phony best. "Parker, take this man over to the supervisor. He's going to be working for us now."

Parker made no comment. He nodded and led the way.

Another fool. Desperate and probably illegal too, from the looks of him. Parker sized the newcomer up as they walked.

He left the new man with the supervisor, ordered him to put the man to work, and went back to report to Mansfield. To turn in the papers and get the thanks and praise he felt his due, as well as the money he knew Carlos and Jorge had hidden. Also his due.

Mansfield was waiting for him. Parker laid the papers on the desk, unfolded.

"No other identification?" Mansfield demanded. Parker shook his head.

"You didn't have to leave any suspicious

marks on them, did you?"

"They went off the cliff themselves. I waited. The current probably got them. Water's deep there. If they do wash up it will be in another state."

"Okay. I'll burn these. Have any trouble?"

"No, no trouble, took them to —"

"Never mind, I don't want to know."

Parker nodded; that was all right by him. His mind had already gone on to when would be the best time to dig up the can of money his latest victims had left. "Who's the new man?" Parker asked. "Where'd he come from?"

"Just wandered by. My guess is he's running from something. He's sort of shifty eyed and didn't say anything about papers. He probably got in a fight or stole something. Anyway, we can use another hand. He rode in on a tired old mule named — are you ready?" Mansfield chortled, *"Mercedes!"*

They both had a good laugh, and Parker left.

Parker's greedy eyes inspected the backs of the makeshift buildings as he walked. No one was in the cook shack, and the men were all working inside. He glanced at the tough-looking old mule as he went by it, wondering how much he could get for it when the time came.

He dug with the end of a crowbar where he had seen Carlos and Jorge hide their treasure can of money. It didn't take long to unearth it. He held it in his hand, grinning triumphantly as he eyed it.

This will be every last cent they've been paid since they got here, since there's sure as hell no place to spend any of it! Parker laughed softly to himself.

The can was strangely light in his hand as he scraped the dirt back in the hole with his boot. Stomping on the pile of dirt, he carefully opened the lid and peered inside.

There was only a scrap of paper in it. He held it in his hand and stared at it in disbelief. It had a happy face drawn on it with a big, happy grin.

Parker made a gurgling sound deep in his throat, his face and neck burning red enough to start spouting blood. He stomped the ground like a child having a tantrum.

"The bastards!" He screeched at the top of his lungs, *"The bastards! Baaaaaastards!"*

CHAPTER FOURTEEN

Oliver picked up the phone with mixed feelings. *I haven't seen Eleana for more than two weeks. She may not even want to talk to me.*

When Oliver got the message that Eleana had been called away again, he was so angry it was hard to conceal his feelings from the old dragon as she told him.

Why can't Eleana trust me to help her with whatever it is that's causing her so much misery? Why all this secrecy? She doesn't seem to be cold to me as if there is another man, but what else can it be? Something's so important to her and she won't tell me anything? If he thinks, whoever he is, I will just go away, he's dead wrong. I'll find out about this other man somehow, and we'll see what kind of hold it is he has on her, or she thinks he has.

Resolutely, he dialed the number. He had told Eleana he would let her know about the modeling job. He felt the heat rising to

his face as he thought of that. This modeling thing was a sure sign she was helpless or
desperate. This was not like Eleana, not the
Eleana he knew. Posing nude was not something she would consider. Not his precious
Eleana. Not under normal circumstances.
Something was behind this, something that
made her desperate. His fingers punched
too hard on the phone, moving a little of
the pain from his heart to his fingers. But
he kept his word and called her, since he
had promised. He blamed it on his promise,
knowing deep in his heart he had to call. To
hear her voice . . .

*I must have been out of my mind, but I did
promise.* Oliver glared at the phone. *I am
out of my mind. And it's obvious, whether I
want to face it or not, that another man is the
cause of this. That's all it could be. And he's
important enough to her to do this!*

His fingers finished stabbing the numbers
as if he wanted to cause them pain, too. He
made a fist with his sore fingers and listened.

When someone answered, he asked for
Eleana. Since he'd called her at work, he
tried to control his voice when he heard her
answer.

"Eleana, this is Oliver —"

"Oliver!" She sang his name, she was so
glad to hear from him. "It is good to hear

your voice. How — how are you?" she added uncertainly.

"I'm fine, Eleana," he said in a more kindly tone of voice, still businesslike. "I'm calling because I promised you I would let you know about modeling."

"Oh." Eleana's voice dropped, her disappointment audible. "What did you find out?"

"That I can hire anyone I want to. The other models are on a list that is supplied to us, but we can hire anyone. If you are still interested and can be here by three o'clock tomorrow, you can model tomorrow." He couldn't resist adding, "The mask and the shower cap are in my office if you want to use them."

Eleana laughed at that. Such a foolish little disguise, but evidently it worked. "Yes, I do. That was a good idea she had. I'll be there tomorrow at three o'clock." She added hopefully, "Thank you for calling me, Oliver."

"I promised I would. Until tomorrow, then." He said it crisply, his voice all business, and hung up the phone. Of course, he could sound cold and all business, he thought. His heart was like a hard, crispy cracker that a harsh word or a string of wrong words from Eleana could crumble into tiny crushed crumbs.

A quiet, unhappy person sat at each end of the broken connection. Each eyed the telephone as if it hadn't said nearly enough, or answered the questions in their hearts.

Well, Eleana told herself, *I will see him tomorrow. I know he does not approve of my modeling. I myself do not approve. But I couldn't tell him why I need the money. Oh!* Her heart ached. *Why can he not only trust me?*

Oliver had called from his office, so he could brood in private.

I can't believe Eleana is going through with this. It's so, so out of character for her. When we met we couldn't even have dinner together without the proper chaperone. Whatever it is she needs money for, she or somebody must need it pretty bad. Or it's another man as I thought. Maybe she thinks modeling is glamorous? No, that's completely out of character, too. It's another man. Always it gets back to that. Another man! Or maybe it's an arranged engagement? They have been known to do that in her country, regardless of what the bride thinks about it. But if that's it, why not tell me? Why can't she just trust me?

His head beginning to ache, Oliver rubbed his forehead. *Why didn't I offer to pick her up? No. No, by George, if she's so able to get along without me, let her get here the best way she can.* He got up and slammed the desk drawer he'd left open.

Maybe she won't come. Hell, I don't know what to expect. Or even what I hope anymore.

Luke was finishing up some paperwork related to the raid he had planned for tomorrow. "I think I could get the Marines with less paperwork than this. But they let me have the men I requested. And these handpicked few are men I know, as well as the Texas Rangers, who have helped us before," he said as if talking to himself. "They're as good as guardian angels."

"That's about all of it, Boss Man. Here, sign this one." The secretary smiled and pointed to the signature line.

"It's not that I'm trying to do away with your job, I just hate holy hell out of paper-work." Luke grinned ruefully at her. "Thanks. I'm going out to the garage now, where I know my way around."

He went directly to the bus he was going to use to make sure it was serviced and ready. The big barn of a garage had been added onto as the county grew and different things were needed. Most of the work was done by volunteers and looked it, but they had everything they needed and a good shop manager. They were lucky to get him when he'd retired and wanted to come home to Las Flores. Luke pictured the reaction the bus he'd managed to get them would cause.

The troops will think they've died and gone to heaven.

Luke allowed himself a self-satisfied smile as he stood admiring it. The bus was an old one he had bought at a good price from a local church because the motor was shot. It seated twenty-three plus the driver, had a restroom, a place for luggage or equipment in the back, and best bonus of all, the air conditioning worked.

He strolled around it and asked a nearby mechanic, "Did they get the rebuilt engine in this thing okay?"

"Sure did, no trouble. It's an International diesel and purrs like a kitten." He came over to stand by it, wiping his hands on a shop cloth.

"Gets a little over ten miles to the gallon of diesel on the highway, and the air conditioning works great."

"Good. You don't have to bother washing the outside again, just be sure it's fueled up, that extra tank too. And if you haven't already done it, put a couple of extra tires in that luggage area. I don't know what we might run into. We're going to be leaving at six o'clock in the morning."

"It'll be ready, sir." He saw Luke hesitate. "Want to road test it?"

Luke took him up on it and drove the bus a few miles down the nearby freeway and back. He pulled it back inside and got out looking pleased.

"Handles easy as a car with this automatic transmission. We got lucky when we bought it from the church and then lucked out again on that engine. There's not much this little workhorse can't do."

"You gonna teach it to shoot?"

"Who knows?" Luke laughed. "Just wait till the men see this thing tomorrow. We've been riding in an old school bus with no air except what comes in through the broken windows, and it would shake your false teeth out if you had any."

"Yeah, I know the old rattler. Old Yeller, they call it." The mechanic nodded, amused. "It's still out there on the lot. And it still runs, unbelievable as that is."

While Luke was making plans for the raid, Jack Kelly was wondering if he'd be able to last that long. He looked as scruffy as the rest of the men working for Mansfield now. He'd got a head start on discomfort thanks to Mercedes, and more than ample body odor and beard by the time he got there. Conditions at the crate plant hadn't helped his looks or his health any.

I wonder what that stuff is they've been feeding us? The stale bread is bad enough, but I'm having a hard time working because I've had to run out behind the building so many times.

Jack looked down at his filthy, wrinkled clothes. *I must have lost ten pounds in the last two weeks.*

At least it hadn't taken Jack long to spot his young cousin when he was taken to the work area and handed over to the supervisor. The supervisor made a half-hearted stab at introducing Jack to some of the nearby workers. Jack grunted at the two or three who looked up, and quickly told his cousin to call him by his undercover name when the supervisor stopped to talk to someone else.

Jack pretended to be glad to get someone's attention and stuck out his hand to the boy before the supervisor could turn back to them and say anything. "*Amigo!* Glad to see someone else that looks able to work! You can call me Jack, that's my gringo name."

"*Sí,*" Tony had no trouble smiling back at his uncle Jack. "Same here. Welcome."

251

Jack had to work hard on keeping a poker face as he looked at his young cousin. He'd never seen the boy so filthy, and he appeared starved and sick as well.

"Okay, okay," the supervisor had interrupted. "This is a working place. You'll be working over here. Jack will be working over there." He pointed across the floor from where they stood.

"Sí, amigo." The young cousin turned back to his work as the supervisor tugged on Jack's arm.

"That's enough introductions." Jack was quickly herded in the direction he was needed to work. A few men watched as Jack nodded respectfully, listening to the supervisor's instructions.

There was no opportunity for Jack to talk with his cousin until after the workday was done and they could get far enough away from the others not to be overheard. The boy looked like Jack felt in his undercover garb. Bad, in all departments. The boy was not only dirty and thin, but he looked almost too weak to work.

"Please, Jack," José asked as soon as he could. "Can't you get us out of here?" The pain in his eyes wrung Jack's heart. He was glad his aunt couldn't see him like this.

"We will get out." Jack spoke softly.

"Never fear, we will be out soon. But, as I told you, I am working undercover. My people will come for us in two weeks. I must learn all I can before then. And you must help me."

He asked questions and his cousin filled him in on things he hadn't known to ask. One of them was about the outgoing mail that Parker took for them each week.

"A dollar for a postcard? He must be making a lot from that."

By the time Luke came to rescue them, Jack and his cousin had all the information they could gather, but they were both in bad shape. Jack had given José the few things he had been able to smuggle in to eat, and used his pellets to purify the water he drank. Both men had given up trying to get clean.

The day before Luke and his deputies and the Texas Rangers he'd requested for the bust were supposed to arrive, Jack's last waking thought was, *Thank God Luke will be here in the morning.*

CHAPTER FIFTEEN

Jorge knew at once he was alive, because he hurt so acutely. With the pain came the remembered look of pure hate and disgust on Parker's face. Jorge trembled, feeling again the wind against him as he and Carlos fell. Remembered himself and Carlos flying free through the air, the wind cool, tearing against their bodies as they clung to each other in their fall. He had felt Carlos still clutching his arm as they reached the river. It was like an explosion when their two bodies hit the water with a tremendous splash. The water was hard, it was cool, then it was cold, and he couldn't breathe.

They broke the surface of the water a long way downstream, where the swift undercurrent had taken them and was washing them toward the bank.

Then Carlos had just sort of relaxed. He began to sink.

Terrified, Jorge managed to hang onto

Carlos with one hand, and using an awkward but swift paddling stroke with the other arm, he got them the rest of the way to the low-hanging trees along the bank. He managed to keep hold of Carlos with one hand and grab a large branch with the other. Then he painfully and slowly pulled them both under the thickest protection of the branches and underbrush in shallower water.

Spent, his aching arms trembling, Jorge opened his mouth wide, gasping at first. He panted, getting air into his lungs and fighting panic as he held on to Carlos.

From their cover of branches, through the reeds and cattails, Jorge could see the river before them glistening in the sun and the steep bluff above the river. He looked up to where they had fallen off the rocky edge farther upstream. He held his breath when he saw a man appear there.

It was Parker. Jorge watched, thankful they were hidden. Parker had stashed their papers in his jeep and returned. He stood looking down at the place where Jorge and Carlos had gone into the water. Hands on his wide hips, Parker watched for quite a while, searching downstream, too, before he finally straightened and turned away. Jorge was breathing quietly, not moving at all, when he finally heard the distant sound of the jeep's motor start. He listened as the sound of the motor grew dimmer. He took a deep breath, relieved that Parker was gone.

Jorge felt weak and his side hurt. He knew he should hang on. It was his duty to hang on. He knew that they should find some way to cling to life, to tell the authorities what Mansfield was doing, but he didn't care any more. He felt helpless as a babe and wondered fleetingly as he looked at Carlos about Carlotta and her baby.

Jorge shuddered, a sudden chill shaking him. He had lost consciousness for a second. He cradled his friend's head in his arms, keeping it above water until it was safe enough, with Parker gone and no sign of anyone else in this deserted place, to try to get up on the bank. He drank a little of the water. He dipped his face in it, his hands still clutching Carlos. He felt strong enough to try to get them out of the water now, though he was still a little shaky. He said a silent prayer through dry lips, his resolve to survive returning full force. Carlos was still unconscious.

But he is alive. Thank the good Lord, he is alive. The knowledge comforted Jorge. He rested his cheek for a moment against Carlos's wet thatch of hair, then slowly, painfully, a little at a time, he managed to get Carlos up on the low bank and pull himself up after him.

He half dragged Carlos, inch by inch. He got him to a clearer spot on the dry land where he carefully laid him down. He cursed his weakness as he fell down beside him, exhausted.

Moving nothing but his eyes, he again looked up at the rim of the ridge. No sign of Parker. He was half afraid Parker would come back for some reason. He sighed.

He's gone back to tell Mansfield we are dead. He closed his eyes.

There was a faint moan from Carlos, and Jorge quickly put a hand on his forehead, speaking softly to him.

"Carlos? We are all right, Carlos. Parker is gone. Can you hear me, *amigo?*"

There was no other sign from Carlos. Jorge rubbed his hands. They felt cold from the water. But he was breathing; Carlos was alive. Jorge laid an arm across him and slept, oblivious to the hard ground, the sun, and everything else.

Later, something woke Jorge. He was aware the sun was gone without even opening his eyes. No, it was not gone; there was something between him and the sun, that was it.

He was unaware he was groaning until a gentle hand was placed on his shoulder. He opened his eyes and tried to see. What Jorge saw was someone big, with a strange-looking hat, then he heard a voice.

"Don't try to move. I will come back for you." It was a low, masculine voice.

Jorge wasn't the slightest bit interested in moving. His eyes closed again.

Carlos moaned, and Jorge was instantly alert. He knew he must have passed out again. His body swayed, as if he were in a swing of some kind. He saw the sky dance erratically beyond the veil of his eyelashes. They were in something that moved. Carlos was beside him, and they were bouncing along behind a horse in a wagon of some sort that looked homemade. Jorge had no memory of getting into the wagon.

He looked at the person driving the wagon, remembering the gentle voice and the strange-looking hat.

As if he sensed the eyes on his back, the driver looked around at them. Jorge saw that he was an Indian. He was big and heavyset with a broad face, bushy eyebrows, and a wide, high arched nose.

Meeting his eyes, Jorge managed a weak smile. It was all the thanks he could manage at the moment. The Indian's eyes smiled back; the rest of his face looked as if it had been chiseled from stone.

He's beautiful. Jorge's mind laughed in a mental hysteria, though his muscles couldn't. *He's beautiful* — hermoso. *Our savior* . . . Jorge drifted off again.

The time after that was like a dream. Jorge was in limbo between waking and sleeping. He knew he was being fed from time to time, and touched and washed with gentle hands.

Carlos was there, too, near him where he could reach out and touch him. He didn't know that he had fought anyone who tried to move Carlos, or that was why they had left him there, close to his friend.

One day the sun woke Jorge, and he was aware that he did not hurt in as many places as he had before. He quickly looked over at Carlos, and Carlos was looking back at him!

"Carlos!" He felt a tear tumble down his cheek. "Carlos, you are awake. Are you hurting anywhere? Thank the good Lord, you are awake. You know, Carlos, that Parker tried to kill us?"

"Yes, I know. I guess we *hombres* are just too tough for him, no?" His strong white teeth showed as Carlos smiled.

An Indian woman saw that they were awake and talking to each other. She went to tell someone and then went to stir a big pot on the campfire.

The big Indian with the chiseled-in-stone face came and peered down at them, looking at Carlos closely before he sat down. He put a big hand on his chest. "I am Naconnah. I found you near the river and brought you here."

"Thank you," Carlos and Jorge said together.

Jorge let Carlos continue. "You have saved our lives. We were pushed off the cliff, that ridge above where you found us, pushed off into the river and left for dead."

Jorge nodded, looking determined. "Now we have to get back to Las Flores and to our people."

"Yes, we must tell the authorities there about the people who did this to us, so they will not be able to do it to anyone else."

Naconnah nodded solemnly. "I have a wagon, but it is a long and hard ride in a wagon to Las Flores. Neither of you is strong enough yet to go."

The Indian woman came and handed earthen mugs of warm soup or broth to Carlos and Jorge. They sipped it gratefully.

Naconnah continued, "As far as we could tell, you have no broken bones, just very bad bruises, and weakness from not eating."

"You." He looked at Carlos. "You have had a hard knock on the head, and you have a bullet in your shoulder."

Carlos remembered the searing pain as they fell from the ridge. He had tried to catch Jorge, then he felt the pain, and they had both fallen. He couldn't remember much else. His memories were like little parts of dreams.

"Are you shot? I thought I heard a shot." Jorge's forehead wrinkled. "But we were falling — he shot you?"

"I do not think he meant to, Jorge. Not that he is not evil enough to do it. But I think he wanted to scare us into falling off the cliff without shooting us."

"Yes, that would make sense. He took all our papers and anything else that might identify us. He would want it to look like we only fell, or drowned."

Naconnah got up and looked down at them. "In three or four more days, you will be well enough to make the wagon trip and you must get that bullet out."

Carlos put his hand on his shoulder. Other places on his body hurt worse than the bullet wound.

"I looked at it, but the bullet is too deep for me to get it out with my knife. I do not want to hurt the shoulder worse. But it needs to come out before the evil festers around it. We will go in three or four days."

They watched Naconnah walk away, big, competent, and in control of the situation. *A good man the good Lord has sent to help us.* Jorge crossed himself and said a brief prayer of thanks.

Carlos said thoughtfully, "I am glad the bullet was too deep for him to get out. It will be more evidence against Parker."

"I do not know much about bullets and how they can tell these things, but it looks like good proof in the movies." Jorge grinned.

"Sí!" Carlos agreed. "We will go to the sheriff in Las Flores, or whoever are the proper ones, and tell them all that we know. They will know what to do with the bullet and with Parker and Mansfield."

Luke sat on a desk at the front of the meeting room, waiting for everyone to come in and get settled. He had picked ten men for this task. There were two experienced men from Jack's own patrol. Two he had deputized before from the ranks of retired officers; and because he suspected homicides in such a deserted, cut-off place, he asked for six seasoned Texas Rangers he had worked with before to help in this bust.

Every one of them was worth all the paper-work, no matter how much he'd griped about it.

He watched them as they came in. They brought with them the weapons they were familiar with, plus the things that had been issued to them. All were good, seasoned by hard experience, lawmen. Luke was grateful for them. He mentally promised Jack they wouldn't let him down as he went over the equipment he had put in the bus.

As they rose to leave, Luke told the men a little self-consciously, "I've got a surprise for you." But he stopped there, waiting for them to see the bus for themselves.

A couple of the volunteers who knew him best wondered at the grin Luke couldn't keep from showing.

The mechanic had washed the bus again and had it fueled, and it faced the door of the station. It was "ready to roll" as he had promised Luke.

Luke heard the men murmuring as they looked the bus over and stepped across to open the door.

"We are looking at about a two-and-a-half- or three-hour ride north, and we're going in air-conditioned comfort." Luke announced it with pride and satisfaction.

He turned on the engine and let the air

conditioning cool a little as they checked out the restroom and the other amenities. Most of them, he noticed, had elected to keep their hand weapons with them rather than putting them in the back with the other things.

Then they were off in comfort and high spirits, Luke hoping this raid would solve some, if not all, of the missing person cases and wondering what evidence Jack might have managed to get for him.

The ride was uneventful and decidedly more comfortable than the old school bus the men had been expecting. They made good time and had no trouble finding the place.

There isn't much of anything else to confuse it with, Luke observed mentally, again thinking of Jack and his cousin. He smiled to himself, remembering Jack setting out on Mercedes.

They approached as quietly as possible, moving more slowly as they got closer. Luke stopped and let his men off near the small outer building that was Mansfield's office, and he backed the bus a little way from the buildings in case stray bullets flew. He was fond of that new bus.

Glancing around, he saw the old mule tethered at the back. He looked sheepishly at one of the Rangers he knew, who laughed silently, knowing Luke was trying to keep that air-conditioned bus out of the line of fire.

Mansfield was sitting at the desk in his office when he heard the Rangers arrive. Surprised, he tried without much success to put on a welcome, displaying his phony smile and trying to keep up an innocent front.

Telling him only that they were making a routine check, they brought Mansfield with them to the work area. Even the men who had papers looked like illegal aliens at that point, and Luke spotted the man who was in charge.

The scent around the place hadn't prepared them for what they found. When Luke saw Jack, it took a couple of seconds to recognize him because of the shape he was in. Even his welcoming grin was a ghost of its former self.

Luke gestured at Mansfield and barked, "Handcuff that man," between his teeth.

He saw the boy who must be Jack's cousin go to his side, and Jack's arm went around his shoulders. He sent Jack and his cousin out to the bus to get water and something to eat from the food and snacks they had on the bus, then lined up the men to check their papers.

Parker had heard the bus arrive and had started to come in from the back. Seeing the Rangers and Luke lining up the workers, Parker moved faster than a fox flushed by hunters. He tried to duck out a side door when he saw the rest of the patrol coming in, but he was stopped by a Ranger covering the door.

With the inspection well under way, Luke went out and looked at the cook shed. He inspected the open-air showers, and the one outhouse because he had to. It was required in the report. It made him sick.

"The poor devils. It couldn't have been this bad where they came from."

He went out to talk to Jack while the rest of the men were being checked and some of them given emergency treatment. Jack told him that several men had disappeared before he got there. No one knew what had happened to them. Some men that his cousin had talked to were going to complain to Mansfield about the conditions. That was all they knew.

"What made them come out here with Mansfield? Did he promise them more money? One of those double-your-present-pay scams like we thought?"

"Luke, Mansfield was promising twice

what they were getting in Las Flores. And he lied about this place too. He said it was near where they could go somewhere to eat if they didn't like the food here. The food. Now there's a compliment, to call the stuff they gave us food."

Luke looked him over. "Yeah. I can tell about the food just by looking at you." He nodded. "It looks like there wasn't water to wash with either. I tried those taps. Those outdoor showers don't work."

"I don't know if you could make it stick or not, but a few of the men died because of the conditions here. It was homicide, whether you call it that or not. It was just slower than a bullet in the head. They buried the bodies out the other side of the office back there. Or at least, that's what one of the men told me."

"We'll look into that, you can bet on it. But that's just a few of the men. You say the others just disappeared? Had all of them mentioned they were going to complain to Mansfield?"

"Yes, all of them I've heard about. They were the ones who had their papers in order. That's what made them brave enough to complain."

"What did he actually pay them?"

"The first couple of weeks, they got paid

twice what they were getting in Las Flores, just like he said. Then he made up some story about the payroll being stolen, and then kept lying about the money until most of them were too weak or too desperate to keep asking about it. I guess it would have turned out that none of the legitimate workers would have survived much longer. It looks pretty bad. Heck, Luke, look at us."

Luke went into Mansfield's office and took everything that looked like a written record. He also took Polaroid pictures of the cook shed, the shed where the men slept, and the area where there might be bodies of some of the men that were missing.

Mansfield made up in his own comfort and transportation what the workplace lacked. He had a sixteen-passenger van and the jeep that Parker liked to drive. There were more than twenty or thirty men in all to take back to Las Flores. The old school bus Mansfield had used to bring the men to the workplace wouldn't run at all.

Luke put Mansfield and Parker in the back of the jeep and took the canvas off the top. He made sure he had them handcuffed in the hot sun, assigned a driver and a guard to them, and put them in front of the caravan.

"I want to watch you *sweat,*" Luke told Mansfield, checking his handcuffs. Mansfield and Parker were already sweating from a lot more than the sun.

He assigned a driver and two guards to the men he put in the van, and he put the rest in the bus.

The jeep was in front, then the bus, and the van brought up the rear. Luke looked to see that everything was loaded, making a silent promise to those they were probably leaving buried in shallow graves, before he climbed into the bus to get started. He also sent someone to see that Mercedes had water till they could send for her.

Once in a while on the way back, Luke glanced over at Jack, who sat with his head back and his eyes closed. He made a note to get him checked at the hospital and make him take a few days off when they got back.

But first, we'll nail these slimy customers.

His smile didn't reach his eyes as he grimly watched the jeep in front of him. Mansfield and Parker were bouncing up and down on the rough road.

They'll be burned pretty good by the time we get home.

On the way back to Las Flores, they only passed one vehicle. It was a rough-looking wagon with an Indian driving it and had a couple of passengers lying in the back.

CHAPTER SIXTEEN

Matt kept looking around the park. Watching the boys warm up for the game, he knew he had more than enough for two teams. Some of them had shown marked improvement since they had been playing at the park.

Juan had gotten permission from Carlotta to go to the park and watch the game that was to start at four.

"I do not talk to anyone, except to just say thank you to play sometimes. If I am asked," he had told her wistfully.

"Well, you know how important it is that no one knows we are here, or anything about us." Carlotta was dubious. "I know you are bored with nothing to do while we are here at the clinic. But I guess it is all right, if you are careful." She stressed the "careful."

"Oh, I will be careful. And I will come straight back as soon as the game is over."

"Juan," Carlotta called to him. He was already at the door. "Eat something before you go, even if it's a hot dog on the way. Do it, now!"

"I will. I will." He paused half a second. "And I will come to the clinic and let you know when I am back!"

Carlotta's gaze was on the empty doorway, and she worried in spite of all his assurances.

I will pray for him. For all of us. And Carlos. Why have we not heard from him? It is not like him not to let us know where he is. I have been worried about his finding out I came here to have our baby, but, now, oh, where can he be?

She looked at the phone beside the bed. In her heart she knew Eleana would have called if she had heard any news or if Raquel had heard from Carlos. *No matter. I will call and talk with her.*

The phone on Eleana's desk was ringing when she got back from making some copies. She picked it up, wondering if it might be Oliver. Perhaps something about the modeling job. She clung to hope. She took a deep breath and resolved to sound unconcerned. But it was Carlotta's voice she heard.

"Carlotta! Is something wrong? Are you

and the baby all right?"

"Yes, we are all right. Juan has gone to the park to watch a ballgame." She hesitated. "It's just that — Eleana, I am so worried about Carlos. We should have heard from him by now. He knows when our little one was due. This is not like him, Eleana. Do you think something might have happened to him?"

"No, Carlotta. He has proper papers, and Jorge is with him. He may have gotten a chance to make more money somewhere and just hasn't gotten back yet. Oliver's friends told us people come here to Las Flores from the neighboring towns to get people to work. That may be what he did. Perhaps he has gone with someone away from here to work."

"But he has not called or written as he does when he is working here. You said Raquel and Paco have heard nothing. Have they still had no word from him?"

"Perhaps there is nowhere he can call from, Carlotta. And you know, he could not call collect to the store."

"Yes, that is true." Carlotta's face was a little less sad. She wanted to believe that might be why they had not heard anything. "There may not be the public phone where he is. But surely there is some way he could send word to us. Just to let us know he is all right, and where he is." Carlotta could not convince herself there was not cause to worry.

"I do not know," Eleana admitted, carefully considering her answer. "Oliver's friend told him there are others, too, who haven't been heard from. Their families are asking about them as well."

"Did the man you talked to where Carlos was supposed to be working tell you about them? These others that they are looking for?"

"No. He only knew that Carlos and Jorge told him that they would not be back to work this season. He was very nice and tried to be helpful to me. I think he is a good man and wanted to help, but that is all he knew about it. They did not tell him where they were going. But Carlos and Jorge are together, Carlotta. They are two big, strong men, and they will look out for each other. And they have their papers."

"I know they have their papers. I know they are together. But, oh, Eleana, I am so afraid for them!" It was almost a sob.

"I know, I know, Carlotta. I am worried about them too. I hadn't wanted to worry you, so I didn't tell you how I feel or my fears. But I have reported them missing."

Cold fear gripped Carlotta's heart. "*Missing!* Then you too think —" She could hardly breathe. "Oh, Eleana! What are we going to do?"

Eleana looked around her. Everyone else was either away from their desks or too busy working to listen. She spoke softly; the sound of the copy machine would have made it hard for anyone to hear, and she spoke to Carlotta in Spanish.

"Carlotta, listen to me. Do you remember my telling you about Oliver? The nice one I have been seeing once in a while?"

"Yes, I remember. He is the one who teaches at the college, no?"

"Yes. And I told you he has a friend whose brother is the sheriff here in Las Flores. These are the friends who have told Oliver a little about these other men."

"Other men?"

"Yes, the other men who have been reported missing, too." Eleana quickly added, "But they are looking for them, to find out why they have not been heard from. To make sure they are all right and nothing has happened to them. Their families are worried for them, too. But Oliver's friend —"

"Yes, yes, I do remember, Eleana. The friend named Matt. The one who coaches at the school and at the park."

"That's right. His brother, Luke, is the sheriff here, and they are looking for them and for the others that are missing. Mr. Lehandro, the man I talked to when I first came here, he is trying to find out where they are, too. He is a good man, Carlotta, and he is trying to help us. You will just have to be brave and pray for them."

"Yes, we will pray for them," Carlotta echoed, still sounding lost and helpless.

"I am going to see my friend tomorrow, and I will ask if Matt's brother has learned anything. I will let you know, and you can call me here whenever you want to."

"All right." It wrung Eleana's heart as she pictured Carlotta alone at the clinic and worrying about Juan as well.

She sat a few seconds after she hung up, looking with such compassion at the phone, the office manager stopped on his way back to his office.

"Anything wrong, Eleana? You can have more time tomorrow if you need it."

"Oh, no." Eleana smiled gratefully. "It's nothing, but thank you."

She went back to her work sorting the copies she had made, trying not to worry or think about tomorrow either. It was not an easy task that faced her. And all that was without the added worry of how much

Carlotta and the baby's bill at the clinic would be.

At the park, Matt spotted a dark head peeking from behind the tree where he had first seen Juan.

A pleased grin lit his face as he touched one of the boys on the arm and pointed. "There he is, behind that tree. Our best hitter. Go get him!"

Juan played with all his heart; he really enjoyed the game. It did Matt's heart good to watch him, and even Joanna noticed him. When Matt stopped for a drink of water, she nodded toward Juan.

"Looks like you've found someone who likes baseball almost as much as you do." She glanced at Juan.

"Uh-huh. I don't know if he likes it because he's good at it, or he's good at it because he likes it."

Try as he might, Matt couldn't get close to Juan. He even resorted to trickery to try and learn his name.

After the game was over, before Juan could disappear, Matt caught him standing beside two other boys and asked their names. The first two gave theirs readily but Juan was already backing away.

"And you?" he asked Juan.

Juan grinned; he liked Matt. "Happy," he said, laughing. "Happy Kid!" Then he turned and ran away from the play area.

Matt looked after him as Joanna came up to him.

The look on his face told her more than he did as he watched Juan run away. "No luck finding out who he is, right?"

"Nope. No luck. But . . ." Matt's strong features frowned thoughtfully. "I've got the strangest feeling I've seen him before. Or maybe just someone who looks like him." After a second or two he shrugged and started gathering up equipment.

Gently, Jorge shook Carlos awake. "Let us get ready now. Naconnah is up, I saw his shadow pass just now."

Naconnah saw them and called them to the fire. "I have coffee here, and bread the women have made."

"We will be there as soon as we have washed," Carlos told him. "We are ready."

"The slope to the water is steep," Naconnah warned. "Watch where you step."

Jorge and Carlos returned and sat with Naconnah near the fire. The morning was damp and a little chilly after their wash in the cold stream.

Carlos gazed at the fog. It was caught in

the edge of the trees like a lost cloud, he thought. He longed for home, and warmth, and Carlotta, and he wondered if the baby had come. He shivered and began to eat. He had to be strong. He had to get home.

Jorge complimented the bread, saying it reminded him of the bread his wife made at home. It was mostly cornmeal and had a few onions in it.

Again, they thanked Naconnah for helping them.

"You have saved our lives," Carlos said simply, taking Naconnah's hand.

Naconnah was a man of few words. A hand on each of their shoulders as he rose was his only reply. He glanced at the dressing on the bullet wound, then at the fading fog. The pale dawn was making its way to them.

"We must go before the sun shows his strength. Come."

Jorge ducked into the shelter and got the letters he had found to take with them. They had nothing besides those to carry, the clothes on their backs, and their grim determination to get to the authorities with their report so they could go home to their families.

Naconnah had put pine needles and leaves in the wagon and covered them with a blanket to make them as comfortable as possible. He pointed to the blanket. "To hide from the sun, if you need it."

He climbed up on the seat of the wagon, and Jorge helped Carlos get comfortable in the back. He put a hand on the sideboard to steady them as Naconnah's mules took off with a lurch. They were on their way to Las Flores, and home.

And hopefully, justice. Jorge felt the letters rustling inside his shirt against his skin.

The going was better once they got to the road to Las Flores, allowing them to relax a little.

Carlos eyed one of the letters sticking out of Jorge's shirt. "Where did you say you found these letters?"

"Up farther from the place we came out of the water. I recognized the names on two of them. I didn't know what the white things were when I first saw them. I had gone out to look for berries Naconnah said grew around there. Then I saw they were letters. The letters we had given Parker to mail for us. The rest of them must be scattered all around there, but these are all I found."

Carlos took the one he could reach. "This and the one behind it have stamps on them. This is from one of the men working near us. How many of them do you have?"

"Six. There are six of them. But there must be many more. It looks like they were thrown from that road above." Jorge's voice held contempt. "Parker must have taken our money then thrown the mail out on the way to town, to spend our money."

He looked at the envelopes Carlos had taken to look at. "After we have shown them to someone in authority, do you think I should mail the ones with the stamps on them?"

"I do not know, Jorge. Let us leave that to the sheriff or whoever is in charge of these things. We will tell them everything we know and where the crate shed is, and they will know what to do."

"Here are the others."

Carlos took them, trying to place the names. "I know most of the names here."

"And we know they were there with us. I didn't find any of the cards. I know there were lots of them, though. And he charged a dollar for the cards, too." Jorge spat out the words bitterly.

"Jorge," Carlos said thoughtfully. "This one here is from the older man named Gonzales. He is one of the ones who disappeared and didn't come back. Maybe he died of the bad food. Maybe this letter will tell what happened to him, where he went or what happened, if he was sick." His face took on a grim hardness. "Or it might say that Mansfield or Parker threatened him. He may be in that field where you found the shoe, Jorge."

"Well, we will give the letters to the sheriff and we will offer to mail them. That is all we can do. But Carlos?"

"I know what you are going to say, Jorge. Maybe those who left, like Gonzales, were not as lucky as we were. I remember the night you found the shoe with the foot in it. A lot of them were gone by then. Maybe Parker killed them all, like he tried to kill us. He did his best to kill us, forcing us off that cliff."

"I know that he is evil enough to have killed them all. While I was holding onto you in the water I looked up and I could see him looking at the water and on downstream, to see if there was any sign of us. He meant to kill us, and Mansfield told him to do it."

"You have saved me from drowning, *amigo*."

"You tried to keep me from falling is why Parker shot at you. When we hit the water, your head hit an outcrop of rock or hard clay and you had a bullet in your shoulder, but I was about finished, too, by the time we got out of the water. It was Naconnah who saved us both."

Their eyes turned to the broad back ahead of them on the wagon seat. Naconnah had not turned or looked back since they left, but kept the two old mules going steadily along.

Carlos was weak and dozed off, still holding the letters. Jorge gently took them from his hands and put them under the blanket beside him. He was nearly asleep, too, when he noticed Naconnah pulling the mules to the side of the road. He heard motors approaching.

He watched them as they went by, envying the speed and comfort they had.

Stirring, Carlos asked, "Did I sleep long? I wonder how much farther it is. Did you see any landmarks or signs?"

"No." Jorge smiled. "Just a busload of *turistas* or students, in a bus, I don't know where they were going, and I don't know where we are or how far it is now."

Naconnah heard them talking. He turned his head slightly, still watching the road. "Maybe an hour now," he said.

Jorge nodded, forgetting that Naconnah couldn't see him. He looked for the water Naconnah had put in the wagon when they left. He gave Carlos a drink and got up on his knees to approach Naconnah's back.

"Do you want a drink, Naconnah?"

"No. I do not want it."

Jorge sat back down and drank, closing the bottle. He moved some of the pine needles to lean back on and glanced at Carlos.

He looked so sad, Jorge touched his hand, "What are you thinking about?"

"About Carlotta. We have lost track of time." He looked up, his face worried. "The baby may already be here, Jorge."

Jorge gave this some thought, wanting to comfort his friend. "Babies, they come when they are ready. But, if the baby has come, Carlotta will be all right. She is there in your comfortable house, with Raquel and Paco nearby.

"And Juan. He is staying with her. To help her, and to go for help if help is needed."

"Yes, Juan is a good boy. You can depend on him. Carlotta will be all right."

"But, Jorge, our first son. I should be there with her."

"Are you so sure it will be a son?" Jorge smiled at him.

"But of course! That is what Juan ordered. Tío Juan, he is already calling himself!" Carlos laughed, looking happy for the first time in this ordeal.

Jorge chuckled, thinking of Tío Juan.

"Those letters you found, Jorge —"

"Parker would not have mailed any of them, as you saw. Some of them even had stamps, and he still did not mail them."

"No, they could not take a chance on anyone knowing where they were, and what they were doing. And we left so quickly when we came here with Mansfield, it is certain our people do not know where we are. They must be worried. And Carlotta, she should not have so much worry now, with the baby coming."

Jorge tried to sound optimistic. "You said Eleana is working in Las Flores. We will call Eleana and she will tell them we are all right. That is the first thing we will do. If I know Eleana, she will be trying to find us, or will ask someone else to help find us. She knows we have our papers and would ask for help. But we will find out about all that when we get back."

"That is the thing we will do." Carlos nodded. "We will call Eleana first. But also, we will contact Mr. Lehandro. He will know what to do about this. We will tell him all that has happened, how conditions are, and about the men who left and didn't come back and the one you found buried. He will know who to talk to about this."

"Lehandro asked us about where we were going. We should have taken time to tell him, even though we had not decided then. Even if Eleana went to see him and talked to him, he would know nothing about where we went. He could not help her."

"Jorge." Carlos had forgotten his discomfort as he tried to formulate a plan of action. "You know how many there were who left Mansfield's place and didn't come back. There were so many of them. There must be others who are looking for their men, their families trying to find them. And the ones with no papers, they may be without hope."

"But they will surely be reported missing, too. To be found out and sent back, this is not so bad as to not know what happened to them. They will surely ask. They will be looking for them."

"Well, then," Carlos said grimly, "first we will call Eleana, then we will talk to Lehandro."

"First you will go to the hospital," a firm, deep voice spoke as if pronouncing judgment from above.

Naconnah glanced briefly over his shoulder. "I will take you to the hospital. That bullet must come out, and the swelling in Jorge's wrist means there's a little crack. I

286

have seen them before. Fractures. That is what the clinic doctor calls them. You can ask someone to call for you while you are being treated."

This was a long speech for Naconnah and they did not interrupt him. His voice held the finality of a tombstone. It would be as he said: first, the hospital and treatment.

CHAPTER SEVENTEEN

The day had come. There was no way to put it off short of canceling it, and she could not do that. Today Eleana would model for Oliver's art class at the college. She got a terrible sinking feeling in her stomach just thinking about it. She tried to ignore the strange feelings the modeling and the strangeness between her and Oliver had caused. There was also the feeling that a cold wind of fear was blowing like a fan between her aching heart and the butterflies in her stomach. The shame at the very thought of posing nude before all those strangers in the art class made her look longingly at the phone. Surely, Oliver couldn't be any more upset with her than he already was if she called and cancelled. *No. I cannot do this at the last minute. I have given my word.*

The hand in which she held a sheaf of papers trembled slightly and she put them down on her desk.

She hadn't talked to Oliver since she told him she would take the modeling job. She was tortured by memories of their conversation as she put things carefully away in her desk drawer. Oliver's voice had sounded so cold and businesslike when he called to tell her about the modeling job. And after all, it was business, she admitted with a pang of conscience. The modeling paid well and was the only way she could get money to help Carlotta.

At two o'clock she left the office, feeling guilty about not finishing very much of her work that morning since she left early. Eleana was torn with anxiety about Carlotta and the baby and the modeling, which she could not bear to think of. She giggled nervously when she pictured the sunglasses and the shower cap Oliver had reminded her of, though humor was the last thing she was feeling at the moment. It hurt to think of what she was going to do. Of Oliver and the way he had sounded. His coldness because he did not, could not, understand.

Oh, Oliver, what must you think of me? I know he only called because he had promised he would. Oliver would always keep his promises. He is a good man. And what am I?

Eleana walked like a mechanical doll, putting one foot in front of the other, carrying herself and her burdened conscience on the course she had chosen. She looked up the street. There was no sign of the bus.

I am afraid to depend on the bus being on time. I want to be there when he told me to come.

She walked so fast to the bus stop, no one watching her would guess she was going somewhere she didn't want to go. Hated to go. There was no one else waiting for the bus, to notice that she looked as if she was going to her own execution.

Eleana stood alone waiting, twisting the strap of her shoulder bag. She trembled inside, wondering if she could really do this. It was coming closer all the time, this thing she had promised to do. She felt as if she were caught in a nightmare.

Only a mask and a shower cap. And of course, Oliver would be there too.

She hung her head and blushed, uncomfortable and uncertain. *If only Carlotta didn't need the money so badly . . .*

Her resolve was wavering.

But I have said I would model, and it is too late to change my mind now.

The bus arrived and pulled over to the curb. She took a seat near the driver at the front.

"I would like to get off at the college, please."

She met the driver's eyes in his rearview mirror. She noticed he was the same driver who had driven the bus when she went out to visit Oliver. He smiled in recognition.

She managed to return his smile. He had recognized her. She was instantly appalled by the thought that maybe some of the students would recognize her, too, even with the mask and the shower cap. The thought took her breath away. Her hands twisted the leather strap of her bag.

It didn't take long to get to the college. Eleana thanked the driver and got off. Her knees felt so weak, she simply stood for a moment before starting to walk.

She took a deep breath. There was no one else in sight at the moment. She walked slowly toward the building at the back of the campus. She was more reluctant with every step, unaware how much her progress down the walk had slowed, feeling as if she were in the middle of a bad dream, hoping she would wake up. But there was no hope. This was real. Her legs moved like a robot without feeling. Carrying her closer and closer to —

She tore her mind away, she refused to think of it.

I could just turn around and go. Go quickly, before anyone sees me. Before anyone knows I am here.

She was near panic when she looked up and saw Oliver waiting for her. He was sitting on a bench beside the door. The sun played on his handsome head, picking out the golden glints in his hair.

Eleana's legs somehow kept taking steps as if her body was running on automatic. She ran her tongue lightly over dry lips.

Oliver got up and let her come to him, noticing how slowly she was walking. He stood there, making no comment, hiding his disappointment that she had come. He had dreamed up fantasy scenes of her changing her mind. All of those dream scenes ended with her in his arms instead of stark nude for the eyes of a lot of art students. But here she was. Ready to pose for the class, whether it was out of character for her or not. And for an unknown person's benefit. Someone who meant enough for her to do this.

A sudden wave of rage at that thought made him stiffen and stand rigid and still as she neared him.

Nervously, Eleana started explaining as soon as she arrived in front of him. "I — I'm a little early. I didn't know what times the bus stops here —"

Oliver looked down at her frightened face. *She's shaking like a leaf in a blizzard. She looks as scared and helpless as a lost kitten. What on earth could she be so worried about that she thinks she has to make money this way? Who is she doing this for?*

Aloud he said, "It doesn't matter. The students can start any time you get here."

Eleana couldn't look at him. She stared straight down the hall as they walked into the building together like two cold, dead zombies under an evil spell. Eleana didn't hear the door close, if it did. She didn't care; she looked with fascination at the long, polished floor of the hallway.

Oliver could feel the tension in her and, relenting, tried to put her at her ease.

"It doesn't matter what time you start, just that you're here for the From Life art class. Class will start when we get in there."

When we get in there echoed in her mind. Eleana smiled weakly and walked beside him toward his office, to get the mask and the shower cap, *and take off my clothes!* She tried to swallow, but her throat was too dry.

When they got to the door, Oliver opened it for her but didn't enter. He said, sounding like a total, uncaring stranger, "The mask and the shower cap and a robe are on my desk. I'll wait for you out here."

Walking as if in a trance, Eleana went in. Moving as if in a slow-motion dream, she walked to Oliver's desk and stood looking down at the things on it. She glanced at the closed blinds, then put on the mask and the shower cap first. She smothered a hysterical giggle once she got them in place, and took a deep breath. Carefully, she began removing her clothes.

Feeling cold and indecent, still lost in a nightmare, she was finally ready. Clutching the robe around her, she walked over and opened the door. Oliver stepped aside for her to come out. He said nothing and walked silently a little behind her.

It was a long way down the hall to the classroom, Eleana wished it was longer.

All sorts of excuses were presenting themselves to her panicked mind, her breath getting shorter as the distance did. Then suddenly, about two yards from the closed classroom door, she felt Oliver's strong hands grip her upper arms from behind, and he spun her around.

"This isn't going to happen!" His voice sounded strange.

Silently, he propelled her back toward his office. Eleana was having trouble breathing anyway, and neither spoke until he closed the office door behind them.

Still clutching the robe, Eleana jerked off the mask and the shower cap and turned to face him. "Why did you do this?"

"Because I don't want my *wife* posing *nude,* that's why!"

He pulled her to him and she frantically grabbed the much-too-big robe, which seemed to be slipping.

"Your — your —"

She was losing the fight with the slick material of the robe, and she could feel the heat of Oliver's body as his arms held her close to him and tightened around her. He kissed her, possessed her, his arms seeming to love her body, pressing her to him. He kissed her lips again, her forehead and her neck as his hands moved down her back, pressing her to his heart. She felt it beating as fast as hers.

All the wonderful, exciting, enflamed passionate responses were intact since the last earth-shaking kiss they had shared and the absence of that slippery, troublesome robe contributed so much more it was almost unbearable.

It simply never occurred to her to resist any of this pleasure; only a tiny little fragment of her mind wondered where she was going to get the money for Carlotta.

"I love you, Eleana." Oliver paused, his arms still holding her close. "I thought, a few times, you loved me."

"I *do,* Oliver." Eleana's face was full of tear-streaked misery. "I love you and only you and I will always love you, but —"

"No buts, no excuses. *Marry* me, Eleana."

Comforting joy washed over Eleana's mind and heart. Oliver loved her! She struggled to find words.

"You say you love me," he said. "Say you will marry me, or by heaven, I'll lay you down right here and make you mine before God and the rest of the world. Hell, I might do it anyway!" Temper and frustration were part of his rebellion against this passion of his.

"*Oliver!* Much as I love you, this is wrong. As wrong as my foolish decision to pose was wrong. I won't make any more wrong decisions." She dashed tears from her eyes, anguish in her voice. "I was so afraid! I thought I had lost you, Oliver."

"No, you will never lose me. I will never leave you." He lifted her hand and kissed it. "I love you and you love me," he smiled. "You finally put me out of my misery and told me so. Eleana, will you marry me?" He pulled the robe back around her and glanced at the door he had forgotten to lock.

"Yes. I love you, and I will marry you."

He kissed her forehead. He looked up at the clock. He held her close, treasuring the moment before he spoke again. "While you get dressed, I'll find someone to monitor the rest of my class. But first, I've got to call and get them a model."

He made a quick call and was lucky in getting another model who could come on short notice. He started for the class to tell them there would be a brief delay.

"I won't be long. One of the other instructors owes me a favor." He turned with his hand on the door. "I'll be right back and take you home — temporarily."

Before he got back the phone on his desk rang. It was Matt.

"Hi, Eleana. This is a surprise. You visiting Oliver's art class?"

"I — I —"

"Is Oliver there?" he broke in impatiently.

"Yes, he will be back in a minute."

"Eleana —" Matt stopped abruptly. "Would you just tell Oliver to call me, please? As soon as he gets back. It's important. I'm at home."

"Yes, I will tell him." She wondered briefly why Matt didn't leave a message, and blushed at his unanswered question about her visiting the art class. She looked around at some of the sketches displayed around the office while she waited.

As Eleana and Oliver drove back toward Eleana's rooming house, she remembered Matt's call and told Oliver about it.

"I'll call him from the rooming house. I noticed the old dragon is practical as well as nosy. She's actually got a pay phone in the hall."

"It is better than having no phone at all, Oliver."

"Forget about her." Oliver was full of plans. "Let's get married tomorrow by a justice of the peace at the courthouse, to quiet any town gossips." He smiled. "Then, as soon as we can get it arranged, we can have the church ceremony at the chapel. At Santa Maria de Las Flores." He looked to her for approval.

Her head awhirl, she nodded to everything, but was concerned when he mentioned the chapel.

I can't tell him about Carlotta and Juan. Oh, what am I to do? She sat silent, looking straight ahead, appearing as worried as she felt.

"What is it?" Oliver glanced at her near frown. "We don't have to have it at the chapel if that's it. There are other churches here —"

"No, no. The chapel is fine, it is a beautiful chapel."

"You've seen it?"

"Yes, I have been there." Eleana hedged. "It's only that, we are doing everything so fast." The uncertainty was back in her voice and her expression.

"Well, the civil service thing is just so I can take you home without having people accuse us and talk about us living in sin." Oliver grinned and added, "I put a lot of that kind of talk down to pure jealousy."

Eleana laughed and kissed him on the cheek, her hand over his on the seat.

"Watch it. I'll wreck the car!" Laughing, he swerved as he turned the corner and headed toward the rooming house.

"We will stop there just long enough for you to get your things and for me to call Matt. I'll take the day off tomorrow."

"Can you do that, take the day off?"

"Yes, I can arrange it. It's easy to get student assistants for Saturday classes and, thank goodness, right now the state and government clerical help is taking Friday off and working on Monday during the summer. And I think it would be better not to have to hurry with everything. Just tell them the truth about what we are doing.

And of course, I'm going to tell Matt about us when I call him."

He pulled over to the curb and came around the car to open the door for her. He checked the front porch, but the old dragon wasn't there. As they went up the steps Oliver felt like his luck had definitely changed for the better, and his smile looked like it was going to be permanent as he glanced at Eleana.

"I'll get my money in the pay phone while you tell her you're leaving. She's mean enough to tell me I can't use the thing."

"Oh, she is not that bad. Just lonely, I think is a lot of the trouble with her. But I will tell her, before I go up to pack."

She disappeared and he heard distant female voices as he dialed Matt's number.

CHAPTER EIGHTEEN

Jorge didn't know how much sorer his muscles and bruised flesh could get in only another hour. His wrist didn't feel very good either. The swelling told him Naconnah was probably right about it being fractured.

Carlos lay with his eyes closed. The lines of pain on his face told Jorge he hurt in more places than he did. And there was the bullet that had to come out. He prayed Carlos would be all right. Gently he touched his other shoulder.

"We are coming into the outskirts of Las Flores now, Carlos. There are houses and a few businesses along the way."

Carlos opened his eyes, and looked around him. "It is a good thing there are two lanes of traffic. We are getting very bad looks from some the drivers of the other cars."

"I do not think Naconnah cares. And I am so glad to be here, I do not care either."

Carlos smiled. "In only a little while we

can find out about Carlotta and the baby. Thank the good Lord He brought us back to them."

"Amen to that," Jorge said solemnly. "I already have thanked Him, many times."

Jorge leaned back, trying to ease a few pains. He closed his eyes and let Naconnah worry about the traffic. The important thing was that they were there, and they were alive.

A few minutes later, Jorge and Carlos opened their eyes. Naconnah had stopped the mules.

Both of them sat up to look around. An official car of some kind had signaled Naconnah to pull over, and a man in uniform was coming toward him to question him.

Jorge blinked nervously. He wished they had their papers with them, but Parker and Mansfield had probably destroyed them by now. Fighting the urge to run because he knew it was wrong, and feeling too weak to run anyway, he listened.

They couldn't hear very well what the officer was saying, but they had no trouble hearing Naconnah's answers. Naconnah's voice was clear and full of authority, and if he had ever been nervous in his life, it did not show on his stoic face.

Naconnah said he had found these men,

indicating Carlos and Jorge, in Lost Canyon. They were both bruised and in bad shape. Then he turned and pointed back to Carlos. "This one has a bullet in his shoulder." Naconnah turned his attention back to the officer. "I am taking them to the hospital to get treatment for them."

Jorge could tell by the officer's compassionate expression when he looked at them that they must look pretty bad, and neither of them spoke.

The officer stepped back and looked up at Naconnah, who towered over him. "I will pull in front of you and clear the way to the hospital. It isn't far now."

Naconnah nodded, and when the car was in place, he slapped the reins to get the mules started.

When they got to the hospital, the officer pulled into the emergency drive with Naconnah following. He had radioed ahead, and two orderlies and a nurse came out to help Jorge and Carlos inside. The officer left his partner to park and rode with Naconnah out to the parking lot.

Naconnah told the officer everything that he knew, which was not very much. He told them about the condition Jorge and Carlos were in when he found them, and where he had found them, as best he could.

"Thank you. They will be all right now," the officer he assured Naconnah. He got Naconnah's signature on his statement and put away his notes.

"I will go and talk to them. See that they are admitted all right."

Inside the hospital, Jorge and Carlos were already being taken care of. They were separated and each taken to an examining room.

It seemed a long time to both of them until they were taken to a room on a floor above. At least they were together. There were two beds in the sterile-looking white room. Everything looked antiseptic and white and clean, except them.

Jorge and Carlos had both been brought upstairs in wheelchairs, though Jorge insisted he could walk all right.

Inside the room one of the nurses left and the other nurse indicated a door, speaking slowly and clearly in case they didn't understand. "There are gowns on the bed and towels in the bathroom." She pointed. "You will want to shower now." It was more than a suggestion and spoken firmly. She knew they understood English, or they would have let her know by that time.

The nurse turned to Carlos, "I will come back for you in about half an hour and we will take the bullet out of your shoulder."

"You will be taken down to X-ray," she told Jorge. "Be careful of that swollen wrist when you shower."

"But, señora . . ." Carlos looked so desperate, the nurse paused.

"There is someone we must call, *señora, por favor?*"

"I will call for you. Who is it you wish to call, do you have the number?"

"Her name is Eleana Castillo, and she works in an office here. But I do not know the number." He added desperately, "The place, it is the Mid-State Produce Company."

"I can find it; I'm sure it's in the book. Her name is Eleana Castillo?"

"Yes, that is right. Thank you."

"And one more we must call," Jorge said hopefully.

"All right." The nurse spared him a small smile. He looked so nervous about asking. "Who else?" Her pen hovered over the piece of paper where she had written Eleana's name and workplace.

"Mr. Lehandro. He may be at Farrel's Grove."

"All right." She tucked the paper into a pocket. "I, or someone, will be back here in a few minutes for both of you."

As soon as she was gone, Jorge exploded gleefully, "A shower! At last, we will be *clean!*"

"Hurry, *amigo,*" Carlos said with a chuckle. "I have been filthy as long as you have, even if I didn't know it some of the time." He tossed Jorge one of the towels with his good arm.

When he was finished, Jorge hardly cleared the door with the towel around him when Carlos rushed in.

When Carlos came out, Jorge was examining the hospital gown he had been given. He laughed as he looked up.

"What is so funny?"

"This must be one of the things like they sell at the mall, 'one size fits all,' or is it one size whether it fits anybody or not?"

"Ah well. It is *clean,* Jorge. And we will be sitting in the wheelchairs," he added as he looked at the one he would wear.

Downstairs, the nurse who had taken the phone numbers spoke to another nurse. "I found the number of the produce company, but they are closed today. The office is not open on Saturday. Mr. Lehandro was in though, and said to call back later about our patients."

Again, Jorge and Carlos were separated to get the treatment they needed. Carlos regarded with awe the room he was in, the equipment, and the efficient-looking doctor who came in shortly after he did.

Carlos spoke only when spoken to and was grateful for the attention he was getting. The bullet was removed and placed in a receptacle the nurse was holding, and the doctor began to bandage the shoulder.

The doctor bent a compassionate look on Carlos as he worked with the gauze and asked, "Do you speak or understand English?"

"Yes. Yes, sir, I *comprendo*."

"When you and your friend came in, I noticed the condition you were in. If you have been mistreated, you should report it to the sheriff here so he can investigate it. There are laws about working conditions and other things, and it looks like someone may not be keeping those laws. You need to report this so it can be stopped." He looked up. His eyes on Carlos's face were serious and concerned. "If you don't have papers, the INS will send you back anyway, if that is what you're afraid of. You have nothing to lose by telling the sheriff about this, and it may keep someone else from being mistreated."

"I have thought of that. I, my cousin and I, we have papers to work here." Carlos nodded. "But we were taken to a place where conditions were very bad. We both want to report it. And I am not sure what happened to some of the other men who were there working with us."

"Is the man or men who hired you the ones who shot you?"

Carlos nodded. "Yes. And a man we know and used to work for, we have decided to tell him all that we know. He is a good and honest man, and he will tell the sheriff or the people who should be told of this."

"Good." The doctor patted Carlos's good shoulder. "You will be all right." He gave Carlos a sympathetic smile. "You have a knot on your head and some deep bruises, but there's no concussion and the bruises will heal. You will be all right. Rest and a few good meals will fix you up."

In the X-ray room, Jorge looked nervously around him. It made him even more nervous to be separated from Carlos in this strange place. Jorge had never had an X-ray before, and he was losing patience with the different positions the technician needed X-rays of. His wrist was sore.

They will tie it in a bow next. He fretted, wondering if the fracture, if that's what it was, would be a larger break by the time they got through with it. They also took some X-rays of the most deeply bruised places on his body and legs.

When they were finished with Jorge, he had only a taped wrist and ointment on the worst places where he had been dashed against the rocks in the water.

Glad it was over, he wondered if the nurse had been able to contact Eleana.

Mr. Lehandro was surprised to get a call from the hospital, and he listened when the nurse called back.

"And they asked me to call you," the nurse explained.

"I will come to the hospital. It will be about half an hour before I can leave here, but I will come as soon as I can get there after that."

The nurse replaced the phone. *At least I got one of them. Maybe he will know how to get in touch with Eleana Castillo.*

Mansfield and Parker had been cooling their heels at the jail. Both had been loudly demanding a lawyer and telling everyone within listening range of their voices how innocent they were of any wrongdoing whatsoever. They were too far away from each other to compare notes, and each wondered how the other was faring, and what he was saying.

"Put one of them on the first floor and the other on the second, and just walk off and leave them," Luke's terse instructions had been. "Let them stew for a while."

He was not going to send men to dig around the crate factory until Monday, and he wanted to investigate some other things, too.

I've still got to go through the statements some of the men made, and I haven't talked to all of them yet.

He kept the file out on his desk, and he glanced at a list of the names of men they had brought back. Comparing the names he had found at Mansfield's to the list of men whose families had reported them missing took a while. He was not sure of some of the names, and wondered if they were right. It would take some straightening out, but there were quite a few names he could mark off his list of men reported missing.

At least half of that list is accounted for. I'm sure, by the look of those poor devils we brought back, there will be some more of this list among the ones who disappeared. I've got to make sure all the families, or whoever left a name and a number on these missing ones, have been notified. The INS can wait till I get them sorted out. The ones we got to in time don't seem to have been beaten or anything, just filthy and about starved to death. Some of them may have just died.

Lehandro was as good as his word and made his way to the hospital to see Carlos and Jorge. He wondered how they had wound up in the hospital. The nurse had told him only that they were there and had asked her to call him.

Carlos and Jorge were good workers, too. I hated to lose them when they left. They're the ones that pretty girl came asking about. They must not have let their people know where they were going. That's unusual. I've heard rumors about others whose families can't find them, too. Lehandro's weather-bronzed face frowned, picturing Carlos and Jorge. *Something's going on here, and it's not good.* He hurried his footsteps, apprehensive.

Lehandro entered the hospital and asked at the information desk for Carlos Castillo and Jorge Brazos.

One of the nurses standing nearby heard him and came to speak to him. "Mr. Lehandro, I am the nurse who called you. I'll show you where they are. I'm going that way."

"Thank you. I appreciate your calling, but

311

I'm not sure why they called me." He looked as puzzled as he sounded.

"They asked me to call an Eleana Castillo too, but the company they told me she works for is closed today and I could not reach her. Will you tell them for me? If they have another number, I will be glad to call for them."

"Yes, I'll tell them."

"Here we are." She indicated a door and walked on down the hall.

Lehandro stuck his head in the door, and Jorge saw him first.

"Lehandro! Mr. Lehandro! We knew you would come!"

Lehandro beamed at the greeting. His smile of recognition faded when he saw the shape the men were in.

"Carlos? Jorge? What has happened to you? You look like you've not seen food since you left."

His eyes went to the bandaged shoulder. "Carlos, what did you do to your shoulder?"

"What we have been doing is finding out that we should have stayed at Farrel's Grove with you. We are lucky to be alive."

Jorge pulled up a chair for Lehandro and let Carlos do the talking. They both trusted Lehandro.

Carlos told him that when they left Las

Flores, they had gone to see what a crowd was gathered about and heard Mansfield talking about his place and the work he was offering.

"We should have known when he said he would pay us twice what we were getting, that he was not an honest man."

"Twice? He was offering twice your pay? And you say his name is Mansfield?" Lehandro took an envelope out of his pocket and wrote Mansfield's name on it, then a slash and "twice Las Flores pay."

"Yes," Jorge said when he saw him writing. "We want you to tell the Border Patrol or the sheriff, whoever needs to be told, about him and what he is doing."

Lehandro gave them a serious look. "I'll do it. And the authorities will want to talk to both of you. You have the proper papers. I have seen them. It is the sheriff here you need to talk to, and he's a good man. He is good at his job and they will have records, so you need not be afraid to talk to him. His name is Luke Jacobs."

"We will, Lehandro. But we want you to call them for us. We don't know what to do. And they need to go up there and stop them, before any more are —" Jorge stopped, afraid of making the accusation.

"Before there are more deaths," Carlos

spoke up. "This bandage on my shoulder — they shot me, Lehandro. They tried to kill both of us." He glanced at Jorge. "I know this is a serious accusation to make, but they tried to kill us and I — we both think — they may have killed others. And they will kill more if they are not stopped."

"Okay, start at the beginning and tell me about it. Everything that happened to you, the conditions, and what you have seen. Who was it who shot you?"

"His name is Parker, and he is Mansfield's manager. Mansfield is the plant owner."

Lehandro wrote Parker's name under Mansfield's and nodded. "Go on. Start where he was promising twice the salary you were making."

Carlos and Jorge told him about the ride on the old school bus and the lies about the payroll being stolen. Lehandro shook his head at that. They described the food and conditions, and Parker's taking their money to mail their letters.

Lehandro asked questions from time to time and wrote down what he felt was a good outline of their ordeal. They could not tell him the exact location of the place, only how long it had taken to get there. They estimated about how far it was from the river, and told him about the Indians who saved their lives.

"So the way you got shot was that this Parker was trying to force you over the cliff, is that right?"

"Yes. He had taken our papers, and we had no identification. He meant to kill us."

"I would have liked to talk to this Naconnah."

"A policeman talked to him on our way in. He talked to him a long time. He may have a record of it," Jorge said hopefully. "I know he told him of the condition we were in, and where he found us."

"I'll see if I can find the officer who talked to him. I'll make a note of it." He looked up at Carlos. "When they got the bullet out of your shoulder, who was the doctor?"

Carlos told him and described the questions the doctor had asked.

"He kept the bullet. The nurse put it in a little tray and he knows how this happened."

"The doctor knows he has to report it. In fact they do all gunshot wounds. I will get this information to the proper people."

Before he left, he turned. "I nearly forgot. The nurse who called me, she said to tell you about the other phone call you wanted her to make. She found a number for the produce company where this Eleana works, but they are not open on Saturday."

Carlos and Jorge looked so stricken, he added, "If you have a home number or any other number, I'll call for you."

"No," Carlos said sadly. "She is my sister. She had not found a place to stay yet when Jorge and I left. We will have to wait until Monday to call. But thank you, Señor Lehandro."

CHAPTER NINETEEN

Luke barked at a passing deputy, "Hey, step in here a minute."

"Yes, sir?"

"Those two we brought in the other day, Mansfield and Parker. Take them downstairs to the holding room. I want to watch them together a few minutes before I start asking some questions."

"They won't be hard to locate." The deputy's face twisted into a frown. "They're about the loudest ones we've ever had in here."

Luke nodded. "I'll take advantage of that one-way glass that cost us so much and see what they have to say to each other before I go in."

Mansfield and Parker didn't talk as they were escorted from their cells, only nodding to each other as if they had something prearranged between them. The deputy wondered with a straight face how the two sleazes would hold up when Luke got hold of them.

The spying didn't pay off. After Luke listened and let them stew a good twenty minutes, Mansfield and Parker had said nothing that would be of any help to the police. He started in to see what he could stir up and bluff them into admitting.

Luke made a noisy entrance, wearing his "I'm the sheriff and I'm in charge" face, and sat down at the table in the room. He laid some official looking papers in front of him. He said absolutely nothing for several minutes, pretending to look over the papers and opening a file he had with him.

Mansfield and Parker exchanged worried glances behind his back as they stood on opposite sides of the table. He turned and motioned to them as the deputy started out the door.

Luke eyed them, serious and as stone-faced as any hanging judge in history. "Sit down," he commanded.

From the stack of papers he had brought in, he produced a legal pad and got a pen from his pocket, taking his time about it.

Both Mansfield and Parker were getting more edgy and uncomfortable by the moment and didn't look at each other. Their eyes wandered everywhere except to each other.

Luke started with some routine questions. The name of Mansfield's business and the mailing address.

Mansfield answered, still looking only at Luke and volunteering no further information.

"And what is your position there?" Luke asked Parker.

Parker opened his mouth, but Mansfield's voice answered. "He's my assistant."

Luke's look at Mansfield was pained, bordering on aggravation. "I asked *him*. And don't worry, I've got *plenty* of questions to go around." He made it sound like a threat.

"That's right, I'm his assistant," Parker confirmed.

At that point, a deputy stuck his head in the door and knocked on the frame.

"Yes?"

"Sir, didn't you have the names of Castillo and Brazos on your missing list?"

"Yes." Luke perked up. "Carlos Castillo and Jorge Brazos. Have they showed up?"

"Yes, sir, they've been found."

Elated at the good news, Luke half rose from his chair. "Are they able to talk?"

"They are, but they're at the hospital. And one of them, Castillo, has been shot."

Mansfield drew a quick, angry breath at that news. His head swiveled around to Parker.

Frightened, Parker blurted out, "I couldn't help it, he jumped —"

"Shut up, you fool," Mansfield snarled.

Luke hurriedly threw all his papers in the box he had brought them in and stepped out into the hall with the officer.

"Take these two back to their separate cells, then report back to me. Don't talk to them, and don't let them talk to each other."

Chapter Twenty

Eleana came downstairs and set her suitcase and a vanity case in the hall, then went back up to bring down a paper sack. Oliver was still on the phone when she got back, and she went to stand beside him.

"Thanks, we'll see you there." Oliver ended his conversation with Matt. He looked serious.

"What is it?" Eleana asked nervously. Oliver had a strange look on his face that wasn't anger, but it wasn't pleasant either. *Matt. Is there something wrong with Matt?* Eleana pictured Matt's good-natured grin.

"Your brother Carlos and his friend Jorge. They've found them."

"Oh!" Eleana clasped her hands, but her joy faded at the lines in she saw in Oliver's face. Her breath quickened with dread, a chill in the small of her back.

"Are they, are they —" She couldn't say it.

Oliver took one of her hands. "They are both alive and they will be all right, I think, from what Matt told me. But they're at the hospital. Matt's going to meet us there." Oliver looked away. "Let's go." He picked up the suitcase and vanity. He didn't tell her Carlos had been shot.

"Yes. But please, go first to the clinic and then I will pray for them, Oliver," Eleana directed as they got in the car. She set the sack in the back seat and got in beside him.

"They're not at the clinic. They're at the hospital downtown."

"But Oliver." Eleana rubbed one hand with the other. She tried to explain. "His wife, Carlos's wife, Carlotta, she is at the clinic." A tear trembled in her lashes. "This is what I could not tell you, Oliver. Carlotta is *here* . . ."

After an instant's pause, Oliver asked, "You mean, she's here illegally?"

Eleana nodded, looking as miserable as she felt. "Yes. She wanted so much to have her baby born here. In the *Estados Unidos*. In Mexico, Carlos lives not far from our cousin Raquel's house. It's only a little way. She, Raquel, and her husband, Paco, are making a home for Juan, our younger brother. Both our parents are dead now, as I told you. Carlos brought Juan home to

322

stay with Carlotta, to help her, and to go for help if she needed someone. With Juan with her, and Raquel and Paco close by, Carlos felt she would be all right while he came up here to work and make extra money for the baby." All her fears and troubles came tumbling out.

Oliver sat without starting the car, listening to everything she told him. He was picturing her anguish, knowing about Carlotta and the baby being due. They were here illegally, which was bad enough, then Carlos going missing added to all that burden of fear, as well as Eleana herself being alone in a new job in a new place. Oliver remembered the anxiety and uncertainty he'd seen in her but could not understand before. Eleana's fear for Carlotta and the baby was what she could not tell him, could not tell anyone. He looked at her lovely face, so sad and full of distress. Her beautiful, dark, Spanish eyes full of unshed tears.

"Carlotta was so anxious to have the baby born here, Juan was afraid she would try to come alone if he refused to go. So he came with her. They both — Carlotta and Juan, too — found temporary work at the clinic. And Carlotta's baby was born there. When the baby was born, that was the last time I was called away, Oliver."

Her eyes begged him to understand. There was fright in them too. That look of fear wrung his heart when he recalled how cold he'd been, how angry . . .

"She is the one who sent me the note with the candle wax seals on it. She couldn't say much because she was afraid to, but she let me know she was here and she was at the clinic."

Oliver remembered his rage at the sealed message, but the pieces of the puzzle were finally falling into place.

"When the baby was born, I had to go to them. I had to know that they were all right. I know you were angry, but I could not tell you about them."

Oliver cringed when he recollected his reactions every time she had refused to tell him where she had gone. He listened now in guilty silence.

"I do not know yet how much it costs to have a baby at the clinic. But you remember when we talked about the little one Joanna and Matt want to have? Joanna was so happy with her plans, and I was happy for her. Then she said it was a good thing they have insurance, she and Matt. That they couldn't afford a broken bone, much less a baby. So it must be a *lot*. And of course, poor Carlotta, she would not know this, as I didn't."

Oliver closed his eyes, but quickly opened them. The picture of how he had acted wouldn't go away by just shutting his eyes. He looked at the face so dear to his heart and the glistening Spanish eyes. A tear spilled over.

"That is why I needed the money —"

Suddenly, Oliver had the whole clear picture of her torment and his own childish selfishness that had added to her fears, her burdens. Burdens she thought she must carry alone. He remembered the night Joanna had talked about her and Matt's plans and said that their insurance would pay for her bills. Oliver pulled Eleana into his arms, holding her lightly like something fragile and priceless, but close to him, close to his heart.

"Eleana, dear Eleana. Don't cry. Please. It's all right. They will be all right now. Carlotta and her baby too. I understand now. I know why you thought you had to pose for the art class. I thought . . . Oh, never mind what I thought. You didn't want to pose at all, did you? You only wanted to somehow get money for Carlotta to pay the hospital."

Eleana nodded. "She is my sister-in-law,

my family. She has no one else here. I know it was wrong for her to come here without waiting to have the proper papers. I know, but she is my family, Oliver. I am sorry I made you angry." She said it humbly, his beautiful unselfish Madonna, wringing his heart.

It heaped the biblical coals of fire on his head. "I guess I wasn't exactly a tower of strength, was I?" He put his hand beneath her chin and lifted her face to his.

"But next time you have something to worry about, and Matt tells me women are good at finding things" — he grinned, trying to coax a smile from her — "you will tell me, and you won't have to face it alone." He held her again against his heart. "I love you, Eleana. You'll never be alone again."

"I love you, too, Oliver. I'm sorry I made you angry."

"Shh, shh." Oliver handed her his hand-kerchief. "It's over now. The baby's here, Carlos and Jorge are at the hospital, and it's going to be all right, Eleana. Let's go now. I want to meet some more of my new family." He kissed her cheek. "Let's go."

The deputy came around and opened the door for Luke.

"Thanks. No need to speed to the hospital, though. They'll keep until we get there."

"Lehandro said they were in poor shape, but both of them will be all right." The deputy nodded. "And he said they are both anxious to talk to us."

Luke agreed. "Anxious to talk to us. Right. That means they have the proper papers. If they didn't, they'd just hide somewhere until we chanced upon them. If we happened to get lucky."

"Yeah, they're legit." The deputy reminded him, "Lehandro said they're both good men with good records and are good workers. They called him when they got to the hospital and asked him to call us for them."

"Hold on here. If they're in such poor condition, how did they get to the hospital?"

"An Indian brought them in. In a wagon. Said he found them up in Lost Canyon. They were unconscious on the riverbank. They had managed to crawl out of the water, but were so weak it's a wonder they made it. They both had some real deep bruises. From the rocks, I guess. As for broken bones, one of them has a fractured wrist. Brazos, I think it is, has the fractured wrist. And Castillo had been shot, as well as being exhausted."

"Starved, exhausted, and shot. Yeah," Luke repeated. He shook his head, looking grim. "Yeah, I'm sure they want to talk to us. Parker and Mansfield are already growling at each other. Wish I could just let them go to it and put 'died of ignorance' on their headstone back of the pauper's field." Luke shook his head, disgusted with the two crooks. "Did you say that an Indian brought them back to Las Flores in a wagon?"

"Yeah. Big guy. Old wagon, complete with a couple of mules."

Luke remembered the one they had passed on the road. "I think we saw them." Luke pictured the big Indian holding the reins. He hadn't paid any attention to the men in the back.

"Must have been a heck of an uncomfortable ride. Poor devils. They're darned lucky to be alive."

Inside the hospital Luke and the deputy stopped at the nurse's station to ask where Castillo and Brazos were, showing their credentials.

"As if everybody in town doesn't know you." The young nurse rolled her eyes at Luke and his badge. "Come on. I'm going that way anyway."

When they arrived, the nurse gave a brisk couple of raps on the door frame of the room and announced Luke before going on about her duties.

Luke removed his hat, looking Carlos and Jorge over. The deputy pushed a chair between them at the foot of the two beds.

The deputy sat on the other side of the beds with a notepad, waiting to write down anything Luke indicted he wanted.

"I'm Sheriff Luke Jacobs," Luke introduced himself. He held out his badge as he sat down to make sure they saw it clearly. He spoke slowly, trying to put them as much at ease as possible.

"Your friend, Mr. Lehandro, called and said you wanted to see me. You needed to talk to me about something?"

"Yes, thank you for coming," Carlos started uncertainly. "I am Carlos Castillo and this is my friend and cousin, Jorge Brazos. We have been working at a place the Border Patrol, or you, or INS or someone should know about. The conditions there are —" He stopped, trying to find the right words.

"They are so bad, we think some of the men have died up there," Jorge supplied.

Luke nodded. "Take down as much of this as you can," Luke told his man. "We'll wait if you need to catch up." He turned his attention to Carlos.

"Start at the beginning. I mean from when you were recruited, and tell us everything you can remember."

Between them, Carlos and Jorge told everything they could remember about the lies Mansfield told. They gave Luke the location of the crate plant as near as they could describe, telling about the old bus and how long it had taken to get there. Both of them talked about their fears for the other men who had disappeared, and the shallow grave Jorge had stumbled over.

Luke didn't interrupt. The conditions he'd seen prepared him for what he was hearing. Mansfield's name, the crates, the general location, confirmed it was the place he and Jack suspected and raided.

"There was no water for us to wash. And the food . . ." Jorge rolled his eyes. "The food, we don't know what it was, but it and the not having enough water, it made us sick."

"And the men, some of them did not have the proper papers and did not speak very well. They were afraid to say anything." Carlos's face reflected the pity he felt for the men. Luke was already mentally dividing Mansfield and Parker's worthless carcasses up between his own jurisdiction and the INS and anyone else who could level a charge, with no sympathy at all. He meant to nail Mansfield and Parker good. He still remembered what Jack and his cousin looked like when he and the Rangers got to the plant in Glorianna.

"And the ones we remember who spoke up," Jorge was saying, "we did not see them again. I do not know if they had papers or not, but we did not see them again." Jorge repeated it ominously, stressing his fears.

"He never asked to see any papers when he signed you up to work?" Luke asked, glancing at the deputy. The deputy was writing diligently on his pad.

"No, nothing was said of anything like that. Only that the pay was good, twice what we were getting here in Las Flores. And . . ." Jorge's hands twisted the edge of the sheet nervously. "We were not sure what happened to some of the men until I found the shallow grave, out back of the place. There are probably more men there."

Carlos nodded grimly at this, and they waited while the deputy wrote. "And there were the letters," Carlos added. "The assistant, Parker, he was a mean and greedy man."

Carlos told Luke about Parker's mail trick he had played on all of them and the charge of a dollar each for letters and cards.

Luke let them talk without interruption, glancing from time to time at the man writing down their testimony.

"But he did not mail the letters and cards. We found some of them where he made us jump into the river. They were down there, where he threw them —"

"Wait a minute. One of you said you have some of the letters?"

"*Sí! Sí!*" Excited now, Jorge reached for the stack of mail on the medicine table. "Here they are. We know these names. And one letter is from one of the men who disappeared."

Luke took the papers, indicating to the deputy that a note should be made of it.

"While we were waiting for Naconnah to take us to town, I went out to gather berries," Jorge continued. "There must be many more, all the rest of the letters scattered around there where Parker threw them over the cliff."

"Maybe the one from the man who disappeared, it will tell if he planned to run away or what happened to him, no?" Carlos looked hopeful.

Luke nodded, his face solemn. "Yes, it might. I will take care of these, and there is a crew already scheduled to go up there to see about that place and the area around it. They will investigate the shallow grave you found and whatever else is there to find.

I'm glad you brought these."

"Parker is the man who tried to kill us. Who made us fall from the cliff and who shot me," Carlos explained. "The doctor, he has the bullet —"

"And we've got Parker and his gun." Luke gave them the good news that they had Mansfield and Parker in the jail.

"We are getting information from them now. And about the men who disappeared. The crew will go up there with the proper equipment to search around that area. They will go Monday and begin digging and investigating the whole area. Rest assured, we will find the ones who are there."

"It is a miracle we were not put there, too." Jorge's face was frightened. "We knew we had to get back, to tell you these things."

Luke nodded. "I'm glad you made it back, too." He got up, touching their arms as he rose. He looked like a soldier going to war. "We'll take it from here."

After the door closed behind Luke, Carlos and Jorge talked in hushed tones about what the law might find when they started digging up there behind the shed. They speculated on what would happen to Mansfield and Parker.

"Nothing could be bad enough." Jorge shuddered.

Luke couldn't keep the big grin off his face as he and his deputy walked back down the hospital hallway.

"Parker will break and roll over on his friend Mansfield, sure as God made little apples. And we've got the evidence from the raid. Jack Kelly and his cousin's testimony. Brazos and Castillo's testimony. The bullet from Parker's gun, and more. The digging team will bring in more evidence than we want." Luke shook his head, remembering what some of the men he found alive looked like. "But we can't help that. All we can do is put Mansfield out of business and him and his partner out of circulation. How far out, I think the thimble-wits are going to help us with, from the way they've already started fighting."

"Yeah, they've got all the character traits of award-winning rats."

"There's something else I wonder about. Those letters. I'll have to check into the matter, but we may be able to bring federal charges against them on this mail thing, too. The envelopes were not actually mailed, and I don't know much about that. But we'll check into it."

Luke stopped abruptly. "Did you call my brother?"

"Uh-huh. He was at home and I talked to

334

him. Told him Castillo and Brazos are here and were all right, or will be."

"Good. Matt is the one who put them on our missing list."

CHAPTER
TWENTY-ONE

"Here, dry those Spanish eyes." Oliver dabbed at Eleana's cheek with his handkerchief. "It's over now and we should be on our way to the clinic. There's nothing to bring you any tears now but tears of happiness. They've found Carlos and Jorge, and they're being cared for at the hospital. Carlotta has had her baby, and if they need help with the bill there, we can handle that. Just be glad they were at the clinic. Was it a boy or a girl?" Oliver smiled down at her.

"A boy. A fine, healthy boy. And my little brother, Juan, is calling himself Tío Juan." She smiled through tears that were now tears of happiness.

Oliver held her close again, more gently this time, both of them feeling better. "We'll go to the clinic first, as you said."

At the clinic, Oliver parked as carefully as if it was Eleana who was with child, and held the door for her. He went inside with her to meet her sister-in-law, her young brother, and the new baby. He thought of Matt and smiled to himself.

It was a joyous reunion. They embraced Oliver, and Eleana cried with them at the good news. In addition to the excitement of meeting Eleana's Oliver, Carlos and Jorge were safe. Carlotta cried when they told her the men were at the hospital but would be all right. Oliver still did not mention the bullet in Carlos's shoulder. The key words here were that they would be all right.

"And Carlotta." Eleana glanced at Juan as she spoke. "There is more good news. Oliver and I are going to be married."

"Married? Oh, Eleana, I am so happy for you!"

Oliver's smile broadened to a grin at the delight shinning from Carlotta's eyes. She raised her arms and Eleana went to her for a hug, both of them laughing and crying at the same time.

Juan shrugged disdainfully and confided to Oliver, "Women! They cry when they are happy, no?" He came to Oliver and solemnly shook hands.

It was obvious Juan had decided Oliver was almost as good a brother-in-law as his big brother Carlos was a brother. He generously and silently forgave him for being an artist, since he was also a teacher and able to take care of Eleana. And he swelled with pride every time he looked at the baby who slept in Carlotta's arms.

"We will go to him, to show Carlos his son."

"Is it all right?" Eleana asked doubtfully.

The doctor appeared in the door as she asked the question, and he knew immediately who Eleana was. Oliver raised his brows, not sure what to say.

"Why yes, it's all right." The doctor beamed at Carlotta. "Hospitals are for sick folks, and I see a very healthy family here."

Carlotta laughed, her eyes full of tears again as she regarded her family.

"I'll just tell them at the nursery the baby has a brief PR pass." The doctor's eyes met Oliver's.

"Uh, PR?"

"Public Relations. I just made it up to fit the occasion," the doctor admitted with a smile. "I'm only lending them to you. We'd like them to stay a little longer, then they will be released."

"Oh. Oh, yes. Of course." Oliver nodded, already feeling the responsibility of taking his new family to Las Flores and back. He shook the doctor's hand as Eleana and Carlotta talked softly.

"I will tell Carlos everything," Carlotta promised Eleana again on the way to the hospital. "How we came here. And why I came to the convent." She paused, looking worried. "Do you think he will be very angry with me, Eleana?"

"For about a minute," Eleana said with a smile. "Until he sees his son."

At the hospital Eleana walked with Carlotta, who insisted on carrying her baby, to the door of Carlos and Jorge's room. She then returned to Oliver. They were about to sit down when Matt and Joanna came up to them. Oliver motioned Matt closer and Joanna came too.

"Matt, Joanna, Eleana and I are going to get married."

Matt beamed, hugging Oliver to him in a big bear hug. Joanna hugged Eleana, glad for her and Oliver and relieved that Eleana's brother had been found.

Carlotta and Juan came from Carlos and Jorge's room, and were introduced along with the new baby.

Juan looked up at Matt, not knowing what to say as he was introduced as Eleana's brother.

"I *knew* it! I *knew* it! I *knew* I'd seen those eyes somewhere before!" Matt beamed at Eleana. "They're yours! Your eyes!"

"I remember your telling us about the boy at the park who was a good player." Eleana smiled. "And it was Juan, this good player. It is true, he is my brother." She put her arm around Juan's shoulders. "This is Tío Juan."

Matt went silent, remembering Juan's pitching, until he spotted Luke down the hall. "Speaking of brothers, there's mine. Excuse me."

He called, "Luke!" His brother stopped and waited for him.

"You just never know when baseball will rear its ugly head." Joanna smiled at Eleana. "He's been trying to catch up with Juan, to find out who he is and get him on his school team."

Joanna gazed at her Matt, her beloved baseball nut. He was in an earnest conversation down the hall with Luke. Even Oliver noticed the intensity of the discussion, and a couple of vehement shakes of the head on what must have been important points. Finally, Matt took Luke's arm and pulled him along with him to meet them.

"This is my big brother, Luke," he told Eleana. "I told you he would find your brother."

Matt introduced them and grinned at Juan as if he were his own. "Can I tell them?" he pleaded with Luke.

"I guess so, but you know, I haven't talked to Stanley yet. There a lot of things to be worked out —"

"Matt, what's going on here?" Oliver demanded. "I know what a conniver you are." He regarded his best friend suspiciously.

"Well, you know Carlotta and Juan will have to go back, don't you?" Matt looked at Eleana and Oliver.

"It's the law," Luke stated flatly.

"Yes." Eleana nodded. "We know that. All of us know that."

"Well, here's what I've got worked out if you approve. Oliver, you and Eleana will be married on Sunday —"

"Wait a minute, Eleana and I might have something to say about that. But we were planning on being married as soon as we could get everything arranged —" Oliver's hopeful eyes sought Eleana's.

"Sunday. We can ask if we may be married Sunday at the chapel." Eleana nodded, smiling happily at Oliver. "I do not know, but we can ask."

"All right. If we can. Let's hear the rest of it," Oliver demanded.

"Right. Luke will talk to them for you and arrange for the clinic to release Carlotta and the baby, officially, on the Monday morning after that. After the wedding. And Jorge and Carlos will be released from the hospital on the same day."

Oliver's eyes questioned Luke. He shrugged at how much would have to be arranged, and Matt continued.

"That way, they will be there for your wedding." Matt made sure all of them understood.

"And —" He glanced uneasily at Joanna, who was regarding him suspiciously. "After that we can get the paperwork done for Juan to come back here when his brother comes to work in the fall, and he can go to school here."

Luke nodded. "I don't think there will be any problem with what Matt's worked out, and it will solve any number of other problems."

Joanna laughed at Matt's devious but workable plan. Her eyes sparkled, teasing him, "And you've got yourself a good hitter!"

ABOUT THE AUTHOR

Jackie Griffey's favorite place is a yard swing with a cozy mystery in her hand. She and her husband, Jim, live in rural Arkansas with their two grown children, a tiny Chihuahua with a long list of stuff to bark at, a big kitty who thinks of her humans as "staff," and lots of books.

The employees of Thorndike Press hope you have enjoyed this Large Print book. All our Thorndike and Wheeler Large Print titles are designed for easy reading, and all our books are made to last. Other Thorndike Press Large Print books are available at your library, through selected bookstores, or directly from us.

For information about titles, please call:
(800) 223-1244

or visit our Web site at:
http://gale.cengage.com/thorndike

To share your comments, please write:
Publisher
Thorndike Press
295 Kennedy Memorial Drive
Waterville, ME 04901